Mask of Grace

Olwyn Harris

Reading Stones Publishing

Stock image provided by Shutterstock: www.shutterstock.com
Cover models are AI generated images courtesy of Canva.com

Published by: Reading Stones Publishing
                 Helen Brown; and Wendy Wood

Cover Design: Wendiilou Designs
                 Wendy Wood

For more copies contact the publisher at:
Glenburnie Homestead
212 Glenburnie Road
ROB ROY NSW 2360
Mobile: 0422 577 663

Email: Readingstonespublishing@gmail.com

Dedication:

To my friend Rebekah, who welcomed me to her fireside,
and opened my eyes to see the world in a more authentic way...

Redwood Inn

1893

Jesus came to a village where a woman named Martha opened her home to him. Martha was distracted by all the preparations that had to be made...

(Luke 10: 38,40)

I.

She banged on the door. The wind blew the rain in on her slight frame as she huddled her shawl in tighter around her. The little lantern by the door flickered; powerless to push back the shadows. The wind howled up and down the verandah, stalking her like a pack of menacing dingos. The gloom of the night crowded in as she looked over her shoulder and pounded the door again. "Oh hurry! Come on... please, please open the door..." She pounded the door again when a sleepy disgruntled voice muttered from inside the hallway.

"Coming..."

The latch turned, and as soon as the door was ajar, she flew inside, and closed the door behind her.

"Thank you," she said. "Thank you," her breath coming in rasping gasps.

The man with the lantern looked at the dripping clothes that clung to her slight frame and formed a puddle at her feet. Her long hair, dark and wet, was swept back off her forehead, tousled in an unruly mass. He spoke with a frown. "Miss? Are you in trouble?"

"Oh, so much trouble."

"Hmm. We are not an establishment that abides by trouble. We will not be able to accommodate you tonight."

"Oh, Sir, please. Please..."

Another lantern appeared in the hallway that led to the private rooms. As the slender woman lifted it up, the warm light illuminated a gentle face, her blonde hair glowed like a halo, grey streaking through it in silver highlights. She carried a baby on her hip. "Maurice? Who is it at this hour?"

"Amelia, nothing for you to worry about. Just a..."

"Ma'am, my name is... ahh... Martha. Martha Smith. Please Ma'am... please let me stay tonight. I would work for the lodging. I would." She pulled her shawl in, covering her clothes that looked suspiciously like the undergarments of a full petticoat. She clutched a bundle wrapped up in another small shawl.

"Maurice? You can't be thinking of turning her out? In the rain and the cold. Surely, we can find a space?"

"Amelia, you know we are full. This is not callous disregard for this young lassie's plight. There are no rooms left to let. It is the reality of our position."

"Reality? Pfft! Reality is that we have barns and sheds and stables aplenty if it was just about shelter to be had from the rain. But you are not sending her down there. I think we can do better than that."

"Amelia your soft heart turns to iron whenever someone tells you a tale of woe. We don't need the trouble that is stalking this girl knocking on our door." He turned to the young woman and saw her lips tremble, whether from cold or from fear he could not tell. Perhaps both. "Just tonight. You leave in the morning, before the guests line up for their rations. Are we agreed?" He stared at her severely.

She nodded around her dishevelled hair. "Yes Sir," she murmured. She brushed the hair back again as it fell across her eyes, and smeared grime across her wet face.

Amelia nodded in agreement. "I will get you a pillow and a blanket. You can sleep by the stove in the kitchen to warm up. You won't disturb anyone there. Have you eaten?"

She shook her head mutely.

Maurice sighed. "And you would feed her as well? We will never make a penny if you spend it all on feeding the destitute wayfarers who come banging at our door."

"Now, Maurice. You are none inconvenienced. Take Hamilton to Lolly so he will settle, and I will see to this myself. Just some plain bread and a warm broth is all that is needed." She handed over her son and lifted her chin in a determined tilt. Then she turned back to the girl and indicated for her to follow, leading her through to the kitchen. She stoked the stove, and then left directly to return with a towel, a pillow, and a blanket. "I brought you a change of clothes too. Hop out of your wet things and you will be more comfortable. These clothes don't fit me anymore, now that I am pregnant again, so you don't need to worry about returning them. You will swim in them no doubt, but they will be drier than what you have."

While she was changing, Amelia cut off a couple of slices of bread, spread them with butter and poured water from the kettle into a small teapot sitting on the bench. She heated some soup and spooned it into a bowl. Martha started nibbling on the bread and tried the soup. "The kitchen staff arrive early in the morning, so you can leave when they come in. Sleep well." Amelia studied her face and felt compassion turn over in her chest. "Martha? Are you in danger?"

"Not in the way you might suppose. I just wanted to say... that your kindness is appreciated, Ma'am."

"Well, I am sorry we don't have a proper cot for you. My husband was quite sincere when he said we are booked solid. We haven't had reservations like this for a while, so it is unfortunate you arrived tonight... particularly when the weather is so unseasonal. I suspect that is why our bookings are up. Normally, I could give you a bed with a proper quilt and a pillow. Still. See if you can warm up and rest some. As they say, tomorrow is another day." Amelia Bailey nodded a graceful goodnight and quietly closed the kitchen door.

She had barely left the room when Martha heard pounding at the front door. Martha held her breath and shrunk back into the shadows, listening as Mrs Bailey answered the door. She spoke firmly. "No, I am sorry – we are booked solid. We have no spare rooms here at the homestead to give to additional travellers. Nothing available for three days in fact."

There was an insistent enquiry, but Mrs Bailey did not waver. "I can assure you, I have had no tariffs booked at all this evening. You could bunk down by the shearing shed yourself tonight and you are welcome to look around in the morning for your companion. My husband does the rounds at five to check if there have been squatters who have not been inclined to pay the tariff. That may turn up something." There was more muttering, but the people left. Amelia sighed as she turned the lock. She was not a devious soul, and she was grateful that she was able to divert attention away from her wayfarer without the need of a lie. She checked in with Martha before she retired and reassured her, coaxing her from the shadows. Amelia suggested, ever so slightly, that if Martha could find a way to delay leaving as early as suggested, it may be better, just until the sweep of the overnighters was done.

"Oh. I thank you, Ma'am. I really do," said Martha, as she sat to resume eating. Amelia nodded her goodnight. Martha inhaled deeply and sighed with relief. She closed her eyes as she finished her soup. She didn't expect that soup could seem like a luxury when she was huddled by a kitchen stove at a wayside inn.

Martha knew the sort of people who inhabited these parts, and she gripped the handle of the fire poker firmly. She repositioned herself in front of the stove's firebox on the pillow, with the poker at her side like knight's blade. Of course, she would not sleep a wink, but she wrapped the blanket around her and laid down near the warmth anyway. In her mind... she had already determined... that she would use the time... to... map... out... a plan...

2.

Simmons clanged into the kitchen while it was still dark with a whistle on his lips and dumped a box of produce on the bench. He lit the lamp, turned up the wick, retrieved a bundle of kindling from the woodbox by the door, and then went to the stove to stoke the fire. He stopped short. "Well, I'll be. We have ourselves a live Cinderella... straight out of a book."

Martha sat bolt upright, and her fingers scrambled for the fire poker that was still by her side. She thrust it up in front of her face.

"Whoa there, Miss. I'm not one for hurting the ladies." He gave her a quick scan and took in the pillow, blanket, and other offerings that had the mark of the House's mistress.

Martha stared wide-eyed at the man in his cook's apron and bandana, shrouded in the morning gloom. She gradually relaxed her iron grip on the poker and stiffly shuffled aside on the hearth, still wrapped in her blanket. Simmons wordlessly pushed aside the pillow with his boot, opened the firebox, cleared the ashes into a bucket and positioned the kindling. He retrieved an armful of wood and dumped it into the rack by the stove recess. He started the fire, blowing on the few coals remaining on the grate. He did the whole ritual silently, giving a sideways look to this waif by his hearth every so often. Flames flared to life, and he put on the full kettle. She gasped with embarrassment as she saw her petticoat and undergarments draped over a couple of kitchen stools, and she quickly scrambled to remove them, folding up the rug and towel.

"I begin my day with cup of tea, because once we start, it is all go. Do you want one? Ahh...Miss...?"

She nodded as she sat at the bench. "I have a name," she said tentatively sipping her tea.

"Martha... Smith." That still felt strange, but the more she said it the more it felt real. It seemed necessary to offer some explanation. "I came in late last night and I told the master of the house I would pay for last night's lodging by doing some chores. And your mistress gave me these clothes because mine were wet when I came in, which I also need to compensate for with service. I am determined I will pay my way without taking any favours."

Simmons frowned as he scanned her matted hair, tousled from sleep and possibly a tale of her journey in last night's rain. Why would she expect favours would be dished out to her? His gaze paused on her manicured nails, and the soft skin of her hands. She saw him looking at them and she moved them under the table out of his line of sight.

He cleared his throat and took a drink of his tea. "Well, it sits well enough with me that you are willing to work for the privilege of camping on my hearth."

"Privilege? It is a rough set up that you call a privilege!"

"And then there's the compensation for spreading your underclothes around my kitchen like a Chinese laundry." He grinned as she blanched. Yes, he really had noticed. "Besides, the extra hand would be sorely appreciated. Generally, there is a habit around here, where the Kitchen Help seems to leave as soon as it arrives. Which ends up being *un*helpful."

"Well, I said I would do it, so I will. What would you have me do?" This solved two problems. Delaying her departure and fulfilling her commitments.

He threw her an apron and set her to work preparing the things for breakfast while he began baking the morning scones. Those staying at the house had a bowl of porridge, and a scone with their morning cup of tea before they checked out and moved on.

Bailey came into the kitchen and frowned when he saw the vagrant from last night, standing over a cauldron of porridge. "I thought we agreed you would leave before the guests are served. And yet here you are occupying the kitchen as if you own it," he said impatiently.

She wiped her brow as steam spread across her scruffy hairline like a halo. "I did say that I would leave, Sir. And I fully intend to."

"Then leave. I don't need trouble camping here. We have enough of that without courting it."

"But Cook was so flustered by all the work when he came in, and it really did seem that he was in need of a hand. And I did promise to compensate for my lodging, so it appeared expedient that I help him get through the busyness of breakfast. This way my debt is accounted for. That being done, I will go. I assure you I will."

Simmons glanced at Martha struggling even to stir the pot of porridge. She dropped the wooden spoon a number of times and tried to fish it out holding the oatmeal smeared handle with her thumb and forefinger like it carried some sort of disease. Simmons turned away with a smirk, took a deep breath, then swung back and glared intensely at Mr Bailey. "You mean this is not the help you promised? Well, that is a relief, because if you thought this incompetence was helpful you are sorely mistaken!" Martha flushed bright red and dropped the spoon again, but he was not finished. "You declare you will find me a kitchenhand but that has not been forthcoming! No one turned up this morning except this one. You expect mountains to be moved with a teaspoon!"

"What happened to What's-her-name? Rina... Mina...?"

"What happened? Truly? Am I the one who is to be tracking your makeshift staff like a bloodhound? How would I know what happened? I might as well up and leave like the rest of this rough-and-ready establishment. At least this one is willing to try, even if she is none too familiar with the workings of a kitchen. I can't be expected to do this myself!" he repeated with emphasis. The bandana on his brow accentuating his frown of disgust. He grabbed the spoon handle in his fist, sticky with porridge, and started vigorous stirring it like a vat of tar. "Get right to the bottom or it will burn," he abruptly instructed.

"Simmons! Tell me you are not leaving! You signed on for a six-month stint, minimum."

"Well, if you don't get me the help you promised, I'm hardly going to stick around. I might as well try the goldfields. Can't be that hard if people are picking up nuggets off creek beds like lost buttons."

Bailey huffed irritably. "Any truth that was in this Goldrush has entirely run its course. More and more are abandoning their claims. But I concede, Help has been hard to come by. Girl, you can work for your lodging until I can find a replacement."

She looked at him and raised her chin just slightly. As if his grudging dispensation of charity was generous! "I would be willing to stay to help you, Sir. But I expect to be paid like your regular staff. Lodging included."

Cook grunted as he shuffled some pans on the stove top and raised his steaming brow. "Well, that will be a problem since we don't *have* staff who are regular."

"And I won't be waiting tables in the public dining with the travellers. However, any jobs back here in the kitchen – I will apply myself to those."

Simmons grunted again. "So, you're a shy one, hey? That is a change! The pattern for maids that track through this establishment, is that they spend most of their time out in the front dining room securing themselves a Digger and a ticket to the goldfields. This reluctance to socialise is a point in her favour, Bailey."

"Okay, Simmons. Sort her a bed with Mrs Pearson." He turned to Martha. "The housekeeper will get you some clothes, and an apron." He shook his head and left to attend to other matters that were demanding his attention.

Simmons watched him leave and then calmly turned to Martha with a curious raised brow, and a grin. His impatient act had already evaporated. "Flustered, was I? Inventive," he said, amused. "So, this little Cinders has a story. You don't speak like a maid. You don't carry yourself like a maid. You don't negotiate like a maid. You don't know the duties of a maid. You don't even have the hands of a maid. And yet here you are. You've just hired yourself as a scullery maid." He noticed a look of fright start to rise behind her eyes, and he shrugged. "Your secret is safe with me, Martha Smith... if that is even your name. We have breakfast to serve. Pull those loaves out, so they are ready for lunch, and I will take these trays to the dining room. This lot seems to think that a trace of gold colour in their pouch, is a king's ransom, and it entitles them to all the trappings of nobility." She dutifully went to grab the trays, but he jumped quickly to intercept her, and pulled her hand back abruptly. "Here. Always use a glove." He threw her an oven mitt and shoved his left hand under her nose to inspect. The dark scarring pulled the skin tight as it ran along the back of his hand down towards his thumb. "You will carry a scar like this for a long time, if you treat these tins heedlessly."

Her eyes opened wide as she stared at the puckered scar on his hand. "Is that what happened to you? Did you burn your hand on a bread tin?"

"A burn is a burn. Just be careful."

She frowned and inhaled sharply. She was not used to people treating her with such confident candour. She turned to him in protest, but he had already picked up his trays and left for the dining room.

3

Every morning, as the rooster crowed with the regularity of the dawn light brightening the horizon, Martha was already in the kitchen. By the time Simmons arrived with his box of fresh produce, the fire was stoked, the water was boiled, and the teapot was steeping. The preparations needed for Simmons to begin cooking were well underway. They would share a morning cup and talk before they dived into their day. She found the smell of baking scones and morning bacon that wafted around the kitchen comforting as Simmons worked over his stove with a whistle on his lips.

Simmons scorned the travellers' pursuit of elusive riches on the goldfields with addictive devotion. Yet it was his habit every morning to take the freshly baked scones into the dining room and chat to the overnighters. He would listen to the yarns of those coming in from the goldfields, plying them with his fresh baked goods to extract the headlines of where the latest finds were being made and by whom. And he always checked with them regarding one particular name. When Simmons returned to the kitchen from this morning ritual, he would go back to whistling over his frying pan.

There was nothing exclusive about the guests who stayed at Redwood. The rough and tumble diggers were usually accommodated in the workers-huts on the property, with scant comfort and a ration bag that they could take with them as they pursued their quest. The converted shearing shed was the budget option that held the overflow. The place was busy and noisy, and nothing more than a covered space to roll out a swag. Even those who had the inclination to stay at the main house as guests were either coming or going to the goldfields. The fortunate ones, who discovered some flecks of colour, felt they could well afford the luxury of a comfortable bed and a hearty meal for a night. Those who hadn't struck gold were on their way to try their fortune somewhere else. Others would come by to stock up on rations before they went back to their mining claim.

Bailey had set up an office desk in the library for the Peace Officers to use as a weigh station to record gold finds. He provided priority accommodation for those patrons in uniform who enforced regulations: officials, mining inspectors, colonial militia, or Volunteer Rifles. Bailey's conviction was that their uniformed presence would help keep order amongst the mining riffraff staying at the inn. There was always a predictable element amongst miners who would protest unfair treatment and flout the rules for the excellent reason that rules were there to be challenged.

Redwood Inn hid its history well, and no one seemed all that curious about it. Sometimes, between meal prep and washing dishes, Martha would escape the sink and walk around the back garden. It was a secluded fenced alcove, away from the stables and sheds, and other outbuildings that had been converted to stores for miners to restock equipment and supplies.

At times, Martha would come across Amelia as she played with her children in this private little garden. Martha was introduced to the Bailey children, Eloise, and baby son Hamilton. "Now children," Amelia said with a playful smile, "say good morning to Miss Martha." They hurriedly curtsied and bowed and ran off to catch the ball that Amelia threw across the yard, while she sat on the bench, inviting Martha to join her. "I tell them I come out here to give our nursery maid,

Lolly, a rest. Busy children are so constant. But the truth is that I am so weary of being pregnant, that it is actually a break for myself!" she confided with a shy grin.

Martha smiled. She found Amelia a breath of fresh air. This little pocket garden was respite for herself as well – where she could forget the kitchen, and everything that was dominated by the shiny lure of gold-dust. Almost. On these short excursions, Martha would linger over the flowers, partial to the notion that such an elegant house now served as a common wayside Inn. She thought that was metaphorical. Elegant, dressing down as a common scullery maid. And then she'd go back to the kitchen, dive into the sink and continue to scrub the pots.

One afternoon as they were prepping dinner, Martha looked over at Simmons who sat there whistling in time with his paring knife. "How is it that you are so comfortable sitting here peeling vegetables? It is an unusual situation for a man to be in," she said.

"Do you consider it demeaning for a man to be a cook? I'm sitting in a tidy kitchen, sifting flour instead of dirt. I hold a regular pay instead of looking for flecks of colour in the heat, and mud, with flies, and always coming up empty. This doesn't strike me as demeaning. Just cleaner."

"I meant that it is an uncommon choice of occupation. I have only come across women working in kitchens before."

"This must be evidence of our modern new world. Perhaps we are walking into an era where men and women can exchange roles with equal ease."

Martha laughed. "Next you will be suggesting that women could manage the weigh-station, or be a Peace Officer, or even be appointed Governor."

"Why not? I've met many women who are as capable as their husbands, if not more. If a woman can rule an Empire, why not a simple weigh-station? That isn't a big stretch for my imagination."

"You have a generous attitude towards the fairer sex Mr Simmons. That is not the typical approach I have come to experience. Again... unusual."

"Just realistic. I have noticed that a rooster can crow, but I don't expect it to lay an egg."

She laughed. "And yet here you are... doing much more than crowing... and you have effectively evaded my question. So, I wonder if you will answer if I dare ask again? How it is that you have ended up being the cook here at Redwood Inn?"

His brown eyes crinkled around the edges, as he started to string the beans in the bucket in front of him. "Well, what does a drover's camp cook do when all the cattle are sold?" he said evasively. "He goes to a shearing shed, to be a shearer's cook. Then, what does he do when the sheep-boom gives way to a gold rush? Not many options for a humble mess cook when that happens, because miners are a fickle lot when it comes to parting with their treasure. The style of cooking expected here is no more sophisticated than drover's damper or shearer's mutton stew. It's not ideal, but I have learnt to adapt to the changing face of the Australian landscape. So, this works for me well enough. For now..."

Martha shook her head. "How remarkable..."

"Nothing remarkable about that. It is just necessity and bad luck, in my mind."

"What is remarkable is that you have taken responsibility for your fate... you have not despaired... you keep adapting... and you do it with a whistle on your lips."

"Well, Little Martha... that is what is called being a grown-up. Otherwise, I would be running away, sifting dirt, chasing gold-dust up beyond the hills."

"Oh, I envy you! I tire of always having to be the grown-up! I weary of being the one who is always required to adjust to other people's moods and their unrelenting expectations. Sometimes I just want to run away, and step off the stagecoach and stop having to worry about any of that."

"The difference between you and me might be that I make a point of adapting to *circumstances*... rather than people's moods. People can be petty and unreliable. I would find it exhausting being responsible for adjusting to their fickle whims."

She titled her head and furrowed her brow thoughtfully. "You'd be scandalously shocked if I confessed that I would very much like to, just on a whim, sit down in the dust, pout, and throw a tantrum like a four-year-old child." She said it quietly, blushing at her appalling secret. She had witnessed such tantrums from Eloise, epic battles that would intimidate the warriors of legends. Truth be known, she admired the tenacity of will that refused to stay silent.

"And yet, remarkably... here you are, in a kitchen, also taking charge of your fate, without one tantrum since you started. And you keep doing what you have set your mind to do, with a smile on your lips. That strikes me as being grown-up too."

The frown on her brow deepened. "Or am I running away? Perhaps being here *is* my version of having a tantrum?"

"I think Kipling said it best...

If you can dream—and not make dreams your master;
If you can think—and not make thoughts your aim;
If you can meet with Triumph and Disaster
And treat those two impostors just the same....
Yours is the Earth and everything that's in it,
And—which is more—you'll be a Man, my son!

I think you are showing more grown-up tendencies in meeting your own versions of Triumph and Disaster than many a person I have met over the years. You are not alone, Martha Smith, in this world full of children masquerading as adults, who choose never to grow up."

"You make it sound like I have enacted out some sort of well-considered plan. It could be that I am just adapting to necessity with a fair smattering of bad luck thrown in as well."

"All these experiences are a way to understand who we are, Martha. When we change and reinvent ourselves, we don't become extinct... or the greater fate... not growing up. You say that what I have done is remarkable... yet I am going to suggest your efforts are probably more notable than mine. I am, after all, still a cook."

She smiled. She knew he was fishing for more. But regardless how fat and wriggling his worm of encouragement was on his fishing hook, tempting to lure her into disclosing more, his bait would not be taken. Not today... maybe not ever. She nodded, stood up and filled a pot with water. "Yes. And it is time to cook."

❧

4.

Martha tackled just about any job Simmons gave her, even though it was obvious she had no previous experience in this type of work. He saw how her hands didn't take kindly to the washing-up water, and he made up a tub of a tried-and-tested concoction based on beeswax and lavender oil, using a recipe of his mother's. Martha never complained, but diligently applied the salve, and kept on washing dishes. For eight weeks Martha stuck it out in Redwood's kitchen.

Simmons decided that, of all the staff who had been sent to his kitchen, Martha was different in every way. He was impressed that she learnt quickly and worked efficiently through their daily tasks. Her hair, that had been wild and unruly that first morning he disturbed her by the stove hearth, was now combed smooth and parted severely down the middle. It was neatly pinned at the nape of her neck in a braided bun, and the morning sun that shone on the kitchen bench, reflected rich auburn highlights as she moved around. He noticed her oversized maid's apron did nothing to hide how she carried herself... like someone who was... not a servant. Deportment. That was it. She walked like a lady. Martha never denied the hints and assumptions Simmons made about her having some sort of alternate story... a different background to the usual run-of-the-mill working staff. But she never clarified or elaborated either.

She never went into the dining room to where the travellers ate their meals but stayed out the back without any curiosity regarding their comings and goings. It was well past the time when the maids Bailey usually hired would hook up with some digger and head for the hills in search of their fortune. Simmons decided that he was curious enough to probe a little deeper... to see how far this little woman would go to hide what was haunting... or hunting, her. He set her to pitting and chopping some plums from the station orchard. He went outside declaring he had an errand to run. It was not long before he returned, plonking a dead duck on the kitchen bench.

"Ahh!" Martha screamed as she jumped up and backed away. "What on earth are you doing with that thing in here? Take it outside!"

He said nothing but went to the rack and extracted a chopping clever... and put it determinedly beside the duck. He looked at her expectantly.

"No! You cannot be serious! I am not preparing your duck for the baking tray!"

"It is usual for the kitchen maids to do this job."

"I have never heard of such a thing! This is outrageous!"

"Mr Bailey has guests coming tomorrow for Amelia's birthday. Social people... hob-nobs from town. He's requested a special dinner. Roasted plum duck is an appropriate menu choice given we have a few pickings left from the fruit trees. Most of the fruit has been pilfered, so this is an opportunity to use the little that is left for her special occasion. Roast plum duck, it is."

She stared at the lifeless feathered mound on the bench as if it was some sort of slaughtered monster that would at any time rise to life and devour her. "I... No. I'm sorry, I have my limits. I really can't."

"So, does this mean you want to re-negotiate the terms of your service? I suppose we could do that. You made a pledge to do what is required in the kitchen, as a trade-off for not serving in the public dining area."

"Scullery duties. Dishwater and tea towels. That is what I agreed to. I have done so consistently. Without complaint. But I *never* signed on to be a butcher!" Her lip curled in revulsion. "Ugh! Dealing with entrails or plucking feathers from that thing until it is bald is quite unimaginable!!"

"If you want to default on your agreement to do the kitchen chores then I will need to put you to work somewhere else. If I do part of your job, it means you will have to pick up other duties. Perhaps serving in the private dining room for Mrs Bailey's birthday tomorrow evening would be a suitable compromise. At least it is not exactly the public dining that you said was so repulsive for you. In fact, to have a pretty waitress when our Mistress is hosting special guests... that would be fitting."

"Simmons, why all of a sudden, are you testing me so? You have always been reasonable."

"Dead duck... or private dining room. I don't think this is an unreasonable trade."

"Is there not a third option?"

"No. I have no other tasks at my disposal just now."

"I think this is completely unreasonable. But since the duck is a constitutional impossibility... I guess the private dining room is the less offensive of the two."

"Then it is agreed. You will serve tomorrow evening. You will be required to wear a formal uniform... with a cap. Hopefully Mrs Pearson has one that will fit you." She swallowed hard and nodded. Simmons continued, the line along his jaw was firm and in spite of what he said... uncompromising. "Kitchen maids are required to do food preparation... in its various forms. Although I will attend to this particular drake, you still have to learn this. Part of the job. Boil some water."

"Not likely," said Martha covering her mouth with her apron as she dry retched, rushing for the backdoor. Simmons watched her go unperturbed. When she returned, with her composure recovered, he hacked off the head of the drake, and plucked and gutted it with deft disregard for Martha's pale lips and clammy hands that she kept wiping down her apron. The whole operation was over in in a short time, but it felt like she had been commanded to stand vigil on a public execution that went on for hours. It was not at all to her liking, and try as she might, she could not feel indifferent about the gruesome procedure.

Simmons walked her through the menu for the morrow. Four courses: soup, main, dessert and cake. He started on his special stuffing recipe and showed her how to sweat the minced onions before adding it to the freshly churned butter, melted through breadcrumbs with the exact amounts of thyme and sage. She had the sense that she was being offered access to an exceptional trade secret. She went to write it down, but very gently, he put a restraining hand over hers. She jolted uncomfortably and quickly withdrew her hand. He shook his head and pointed to the bowl of breadcrumbs. "This stuffing is best for game-fowl... roasted partridge, duck, goose, turkey, quail and the like." With a flourish, he proceeded to stuff the cavity of the bird before him with his special stuffing. "The recipe has not been put to paper for at least three generations. It was given to my mother by a remarkable old cook. If you cannot hold it to memory, then it is evident you are not sensible of the privilege you are being offered."

"Something tells me that the stockmen of your Drover camps ate exceptionally well. Or was that a story you told me to keep my curiosity at bay?"

He added some crushed garlic to the marinade mixture in a bowl and began to liberally brush it over the bird now rubbed with herbs, sitting proud in the baking tray. "I did do a stint in drovers' camps," he said as crouched down at bench height, focused on painting the marinade around the wings like an artist with his paintbrush and canvas. He looked up and openly held her gaze. "I would not lie...not to you."

Martha stared at him. The moment was so honest, so vulnerable, it took her breath away. She cleared her throat and collected his used bowls to place by the sink. "I believe you are as excited by Bailey's dinner arrangement as Amelia is. This gives you an opportunity to showcase your efforts. You are an artist Seth Simmons, and you are no less masked than I am with this mess-cook persona you insist on.

"We are all reinventing ourselves, Lady Martha. No one is ever exactly who they seem."

5

After lunch the next day, the preparations for Amelia's birthday were ramping up. The housekeeper, Mrs Pearson, brought in a folded pile of clothes. "Your uniform, Miss. For the special occasions."

Martha took the bundle from her arms. She was not sure she could pull this off. Wiping up dishes was one thing. This, however, was entirely different. She turned abruptly to Simmons. "Don't you think it would be better to have someone with experience serving tonight? I do not want to shame the Baileys in front of their guests."

"Mrs Bailey is the least pretentious person I have ever met. Besides, I think you have experience. Just do what you expect others to do for you."

"But I never took any notice. It was all just there."

"Exactly. All you need to do is put it 'just there' for them."

"Oh. Okay."

He was focused on the serving platters before him. He put one to the side when he found a hair-line fracture in the china and a small chip on the edge. Every time he tested his assumptions, she confirmed them. *Hmm,* he thought. *Little Martha, you and your mysteries are quite intriguing.* "You have done your job well if no one notices you," he said with intentional indifference as he turned away.

As the clock chimed six in the dining room, Mrs Pearson bundled into the kitchen, a clean apron and cap firmly in place over her greying hair, carrying a basket of fresh produce. "The table is set; the guests have started to arrive. Zach and Tibby brought tomorrow's produce, to save the pick-up in the morning. They are all having drinks now."

"Who are Zach and Tibby?" asked Martha, as she smoothed her hair once more and pinned her cap.

Mrs Pearson raised her brow at this gap in Redwood knowledge. "They own this establishment with the Baileys. All the produce for the kitchen comes from Zach... Mr Logan. He has a rather extensive market garden over the way. Kangaroos used to be the main problem eating his garden, now it is swagmen and travelling diggers. Simmons picks up the supplies every morning. Are we ready? They will be seated soon."

Simmons grinned. "As ready as... a duck on a serving platter." He checked his Rhubarb Crumble tartlets and rotated the trays in the oven with the Lemon Curd ones. He stirred the soup again. He moved through his tasks like choreographed swordplay. "Mrs Pearson will take the soup tureen and ladle it into the bowls. You deliver those bowls to the table. Serve Amelia first, as the guest of honour, then the other women. Men from the head of the table after that. Remember... always serve from the left; clear from the right."

"Yes sir." She wiped her palms down her skirt under her apron, to keep it pristine white. "I had no idea that serving a meal was such an event," she muttered. "Each one of my staff deserves a medal of valour." She took a deep breath and plunged through the door.

Simmons heard her comment and watched her go with a raised brow. He quickly checked the large pot of stew for the main dining room and took the tartlets out of the oven and set them on a cooling rack. Then he set to finishing the layering of his Pumpkin, Ginger, Date, and Treacle Stack Cake. He thought the name was like the multiple layers of the cake, all the elements fitting together in a remarkable combination. He focused intensely on placing the tiers, smoothing the filling between each layer.

Mrs Pearson ladled out the soup and handed the bowl to Martha. She glanced towards Amelia as she set her bowl down. Amelia smiled, and nodded, and continued talking with a mature lady, with a heavy shawl, about her heartburn which was never an issue with her other pregnancies. "I just don't want a hairy baby... it sounds so very unattractive. I would love him just the same of course, but I heard the midwife say that heartburn has a lot to do with hairy babies."

Martha smiled and thought it would be an impossibility for Amelia to have children who were not picture-book perfect. She thought of Eloise playing on the swing, with her picture-book flaxen curls, and her picture-book cupid-bow lips. She collected the next bowl and froze. Another couple entered the room, laughing amiably, and apologising profusely for their tardiness. Martha quickly handed the soup bowl to Mrs Pearson and fled.

Simmons placed another layer on his stack cake when he looked up and saw Martha's pale face standing by the door, her slight frame shaking. "What's the matter? Is the soup not satisfactory?"

She shook her head, her breathing rasping. "No, your potato-and-leek is a sensation. Mrs Pearson is finishing serving the soup bowls, so I could get some fresh air."

"What happened? You look like you have seen a ghost."

"It's just... I know one of those visitors from town. I can't go back in there."

"You know them? How?"

"I... they really can't know I am here."

"They won't be expecting you in a maid's cap, surely," he said studying the minced date filling in the bowl in front of him with a frown. He took a spoon, mixing it smooth once more, glancing up at the despair on her face. He turned back to his layer cake, spreading the filling and placing another layer with precise care.

"I heard him talk. He is on his way to the goldfields... looking for me."

"You? Oh. Well." He paused, put down his spatula and went over to her, drawing her back into the kitchen. "There's a lot to do, since we are managing the front dining room as well. And we still have to get through three courses in there. Can you keep going? Can you do this?"

"I don't think I can..."

"Martha, you can stay undetected. Amelia has been anticipating this evening for a long time. Her pregnancy hasn't been easy, and there is not a kinder soul on Earth. She rarely asks for anything. She has been anticipating her birthday for weeks."

Martha took a slow deep breath and straightened her back. "Oh yes. Yes, of course. Mrs Bailey has been so kind to me. We will see that she gets her dessert... and a layered birthday cake."

"Good on you, Little Martha," he said with open admiration. "Sometimes the best hiding is in plain sight. A maid-mask is an effective cover. You only need to help Mrs Pearson. Do you normally wear your hair like this?" She nodded. "Then change it. Make it scruffy, like that first morning I saw you."

"Scruffy? I hardly think that is flattering even for a maid!" She took a breath... and shuddered. All the ground she had covered these last months was suddenly giving way. She felt off-balance. "This smooth fashion is the only way I wear it. If my hair gets wet, it goes frizzy. It is quite a lot of work to tie it back. I can't change it just like that."

"Sure, you can: frizzy is different. Why not make it short?"

"You mean cut it like a man's?"

"If you intend to stay hidden, something quick to give a drastically different look might be what you need." Would she really go to such lengths?

"Oh." The idea took a bit of absorbing. "Okay. Yes. But you will have to help me. I have never done anything this radical before."

He chuckled. "Says, Little Martha sporting a maid's uniform like a professional. I think you do radical more often than you give yourself credit for." He grabbed some shears from the shelf. "Are you certain?"

She nodded determinedly and braced herself. "I go back... on my own terms." She took off her cap and put it to the side. And pulled out her hair pins, and a long auburn braid of hair fell past her shoulders. Simmons raised his brow, swallowed, grasped it, took a breath, and lopped it off above her collar like he was piecing a chicken for baking. He put the braid in an empty flour bag like a dead snake. "You can decide what to do with the evidence later," he said, brushing off stands of hair from her shoulder. "You could sell it to a wigmaker."

"I'm not sure what I think about someone else wearing my hair. And a reputable perruquier is not easy to find. Leave it there. I'll think about it."

Simmons raised his brow. There it was again... the alternate story. Without hesitation. He watched Martha go to the bucket and splash some water on her hair. He threw her a tea-towel. She tousled her damp hair and true to her prediction it exploded on her collar.

Frizzy it was. Simmons' face melted into a grin of candid admiration. "You need not have worried about it not being flattering. That suits you. Very much."

"Really?" Martha paused and then shook her head to dismiss the compliment with a frown. "Well, that is counterproductive! I need to stay invisible, not to draw attention to myself."

"My mistake. It might not have been the best idea after all," he muttered as he turned away. He went over to the bench to finish the stack cake sitting on the pedestal cake stand. He carefully cut out a wedge, so that all the layers were revealed, and put the pieces aside. "If different is what we are going for, it is definitely different. Pin it off your face and put your cap back on. And loosen your apron. It fits too well... and tie a clumsy bow. Then slouch a bit. No eye-contact. Martha... you can do this."

"My name is... Charlotte Martina... Willett."

He raised his brow. "Willett, huh? You really did fall out of your high society tree to end up here. Still, I suspect the Law pursuing a runaway still considers them a fugitive... regardless of where they grew up."

"Do you think I am a felon, evading arrest? You suppose those in the dining room are here to apprehend me?" She tilted her head and looked at him. Shocked. "And yet you are helping me anyway? Well, allow me to reassure you Simmons: escaped and pursued, but no criminal charges. Why would you think that?"

"I don't know... Bailey was agitated that first morning you arrived here out of nowhere. He is usually fairly flexible, but he definitely wanted you gone. Him being a lawyer and all... made me think he had reason for that. And the way you kept your head down, added weight to the idea. Nevertheless, Willett or otherwise, tonight, you are Martha: scullery maid of Redwood. I think we can do this. Mrs Pearson will do the table service, and you only need to be there to back her up... and help clear. We are not plating up the main... they are serving themselves from the platters. So that makes it simpler..."

"And the dessert tartlets? Cake?"

He went to the cabinet and pulled out a full table setting of different sized fine china plates, and some stemmed glasses. "We will use tiered serving plates. Wash these glasses and plates; we will arrange the tartlets on them. The glasses become the pedestal for the next layer. I'll pour the custard into these gravy boats, so wash them too." He put all of the pieces near the sink.

Mrs Pearson came back in and raised her brow as she saw Martha's hair. "They will be ready for the next course soon." They could hear plenty of chatter and laughter echoing through the hallways from the dining room. "Come, I'll take the duck. Bailey is carving. You follow me with the platters of vegetables and sides," she said efficiently.

Simmons went to the warming oven and pulled out the platter. He lifted the cover and revealed the most succulent roast. He drizzled a final layer of plum glaze over the breast of the duck and put back the cover before he handed it over into Mrs Pearson's custody. He passed the vegetables to Martha, who placed them on the trolley. "Remember, your protection is being invisible. No eye-contact, no matter how tempting," he whispered.

She swallowed. And followed Mrs Pearson's stately parade back to the dining room, pushing the trolley. They placed the serving dishes down the centre of the dining table. Martha knocked one of the gravy boats as she nervously removed a dish from the trolly. She held her breath and almost expected Cyrus to leap to his feet to expose her pretence. She quickly tried to mop the spilt gravy with a cloth. He glanced her way but continued to happily chat to the pretty companion beside him, all charm and manners. Of course. This tendency of his to have a wandering eye... and a roving hand, was a thorn in their relationship. But right now, his flirting meant he barely noticed anything, and she stayed undetected. She positioned the final serving dish on the table and made her escape.

Martha stood by the stove and took a deep breath. And then she took another. "Hey?" Simmons came and stood in front of her. "Did they notice?" She shook her head. "See? What did I say, Little Martha? Working class – the perfect disguise."

"That man in there, he wasn't just on commission to bring me home. He spoke to my Father. He wanted us to become engaged." Simmons face was unreadable. Martha shook her frizzy mop. "Father agreed to it. He is in there impressing everyone with his mission to rescue me from the squalor of the goldfields, since they assume I have fled there..."

"Why would they assume that?"

She frowned slightly, intrigued that he would ask about that, and not demand details on the impending betrothal. "I might have fed the idea to them... a little. I dropped some comments about the flood of good fortune stories... the excitement... the adventure..."

"And yet you never had any intention of going there," he observed.

She shuddered. "It was a decoy. I might be bold enough to cut off my hair... but sleeping on the ground under makeshift canvas tents while everyone around scrapes around in the dirt and dust and mud?

Aargh! Like you, I prefer cleaner adventures. A warm hearth with a blanket... for one night only, is my limit on daring. I am not as brave as you try to make me, Simmons."

"So, this man who is in there eating our food, it seems your father considers him worthy, but you doubt your family's wisdom in this choice for you?"

"His name is Cyrus. Cyrus Dempsey. He has a good family, and he gave such pretty speeches to Father... and to me... about the expediency of the match. Yet he is in there flirting shamelessly, declaring his broken heart, no doubt, to the limpid eyes of his sympathetic audience of one. Still, my father likes him well enough. I might..."

Simmons was watching her carefully. "You might? Oh no! Please don't tell me you intend to marry the guy?" *Oh, Little Martha, you deserve more. So much more.*

She shook her head in disgust. "I was going to say, I *might* have just gone along with what was recommended. I usually do. My father generally has my best in mind. But..." She shrugged.

"But... now he is exposed as a shallow, no good, worthless philanderer."

"Yes, there is that... *but...* I have already met someone. I am already in love with another. I could never marry Cyrus under these circumstances. I know my love will not be considered a suitable match, and I know my Father would never agree to it... so I am finding a different path."

His heart leaped in hope. "This other fellow... is he so shocking?"

"He is."

"You don't strike me as a reckless woman Little Martha. What makes him such a violation of your family's sensibility?"

"The violation is simply a matter of birth. He is a nobody, with no pedigree."

"Oh?" His eyes softly watched her struggle. But before he could reassure her, she continued without pause.

"His family is French. A hound would have better credentials."

Simmons inhaled quickly and felt his heart sink on two accounts, but he turned away and held himself firm. "Oh. French. And that is how he stole your loyalty and affection? Because your family would not approve? There is a rebel in you after all."

"No, of course not. What commends Edwin to my heart is that he is charming and considerate, intentional and thoughtful, skilled and masterful at what he does. It is not fair that his lack of English lineage prohibits us from each other."

She would have gone on, but Simmons picked up a spoon and focused intently on thinning the treacle sauce that would be poured over his cake as it was presented. He frowned, took it off the heat and whisked the mixture smooth. "Well, now that the main course is served, there is no need to expose you to further risk. The social group in the dining room have eaten down to dessert; they are filled and relaxed. I can help Mrs Pearson take out the tartlets... and then the cake... and there are already mounds of stacked dishes for you to attend to. You can stay safely hidden back here behind your mountain of washing-up."

"Thank you, Simmons. Thank you!" She sprung up and gave him a hug.

"No need to thank me. The dishes thank you," he said stiffly without even blinking.

"I mean to thank you for your kindness to shield me. That is a great service. I just need to stay hidden a while longer. Cyrus will be gone in the morning no doubt... and I know that when Edwin comes as we agreed, I can put this behind me. Once we are married, I know my father will come to like Edwin as much as I do. We are meeting up here in two months. This was our plan."

"Hmm. So, this is why you have not flown off into the craggy rocks of gold mining like everyone else. You are on a timeline. That also explains why you so impudently hired yourself here at Redwood. You have a determined, loyal heart, Little Martha. Still, two months on every account is unsatisfactory."

"Unsatisfactory? What do you mean?"

"Dempsey is in there, comfortably eating our food, trifling with another's heart while you are missing. The time he has taken as a thwarted intended to recover his future wife... is ridiculously belated. It is the mark of a deserter. He would be shot by a firing squad for such a crime in any other setting. But two months for a man in love is also impossibly tardy. Edwin's devotion sounds merely convenient, and your absence appears to be no bother for him. I think you are worth more on both accounts."

She laughed. "Simmons, you are just like my father. He is also impossible to please."

"I disagree Martha. I am different to your father on at least two accounts. Firstly, I am not old enough, and secondly, I am adequately pleased." He had not taken his eyes off the saucepan, focused intently on his task even as he spoke.

Mrs Pearson appeared with some of the serving bowls. "I am about to clear the plates from the main course. Simmons, the accolades for your dishes are again pouring forth. Satisfaction is at an all-time high."

"Well let's get these tartlets to them, to stall any undoing of their contentment. Martha... start the washing up." He sat the pan on a trivet, took off his apron and picked up the stemmed glasses and plate, and Mrs Pearson followed with the rest.

Martha stared after him and frowned. She was surprised Simmons was so serious about her confessions. She had assumed the whole drama would be an amusing distraction from his mundane kitchen routines. She thought he might even say those predictable words, *'I knew it! I knew all along there was more!'* Yet nothing changed in his manner with her.

Simmons walked into the dining room with a flourish. He set the plates on the stemmed glasses and arranged his delicious desserts creating a tiered centrepiece. Amelia stood up and clapped. Every eye turned towards him. "This is the master of this evening's fare. Let me introduce to you, our cook, Seth Simmons. It is very fortunate that we have someone with such diverse talents. He can manage the routine cooking for travellers and then turn his hand to the art we have experienced this evening."

He nodded. "You are gracious, Ma'am."

"Pfft. It is true. You hardly ever have the opportunity to showcase your true capabilities. Damper and Bully Stew seem too ordinary."

"Ordinary is the stuff of life. This is the icing on the cake. Which brings me to my next offering. Ladies... save something in your waistlines for a very special treat," he said with charm. "The birthday cake is still to come..."

"Oooh! That does sound exciting. Tonight, has been a perfect delight. We are grateful Simmons." And Amelia glowingly showered her appreciation on her husband, who stood with an invitation for their guests to charge their glasses, and he proceeded to offer a toast.

Simmons quickly identified which guest was the philandering Cyrus Dempsey. He smoothed the frown that instantly furrowed his brow. He was relieved that Martha was saved from his clutches. He had no prick of conscience that the young woman sitting beside Dempsey, smiling so eagerly, should likewise be rescued. She served as the bait of distraction. All the more convenient since it was of her own choosing. He nodded and made his exit as they started to serve the tartlets, drizzling them with cream custard.

When he came through the kitchen door, Martha was still standing at the bench where he had left her. She had not moved to start the dishes. He rubbed his forehead hard under the hem of his bandana and felt the tension on his shoulders knot tighter. He stood for a moment watching the look on her face. He came to her side, and she turned and reached out and grabbed his forearm, seeking to be stabilized. "Why should his behaviour hurt so, when I have no intention of going ahead with the engagement?"

Simmons pulled a stool to the bench and sat her down. He plied her with a freshly brewed coffee, and a portion of a lemon curd tartlet that had broken while he was arranging them.

She had no heart to resist his kindness. "Oh Simmons. If I had not escaped to interrupt their expectations, that wedding would really have gone ahead. But I know Cyrus. It would never be about us. He would be bored of me within a week and make a mockery of our vows with the next floozie who smiles at him. Why would he even bother Father to secure consent for my hand?"

"A man like that? There is only one thing that makes sense. He's like every other miner who passes through here. It is easy enough to identify a gold-digger when he pushes a barrow filled with gold-pans, a pick, and a shovel. But when the tool of choice is a charming smile, and respectable social credentials, he is harder to spot. You cannot blame yourself for the deception your family was subjected to. You did well to discern the truth."

"See! Why do you do that? I want you say something insensitive and harsh, so I can be mad at you too. But you are straight forward and kind." She sighed. "Still, I know you are right."

"You can be angry. It is wrong that he has mistreated your family's trust. But I have no need to join the ranks of men who are behaving badly. So, direct your anger at its rightful target, and allow me to be your friend."

"Yes! You are right! He did behave poorly!" She jumped up from the bench. Simmons quietly stood up and closed the kitchen door discretely as she paced around the kitchen. "And still he is out there behaving badly!" she cried. She leant her back against the wall... and slid down until she was sitting on the flagstone floor. "So badly..." she whimpered, confused.

Simmons came and sat beside her. "He did, Little Martha. He did. Anyone who justifies their bad behaviour by assuming your station and influence holds more value than your heart, is not worthy of your hand."

"Am I so dull? It is true, isn't it? At home the social pages report I am the village idiot who is tolerated because I have a nice wardrobe.

Here I am, acting the role of a dull handmaiden who is ignored because a service apron makes me invisible. It is just another mask that hides the truth. No one sees who I truly am..."

"You have shown courage, perseverance, and devotion. How is that dull? This maid-mask that you wear, has revealed that truth... not hidden it. At least to me."

"It seems it is the pattern. Charlotte Willett... dense and dull."

"Well, it is my privilege that I met Martha first. She is a lady who is daring and discerning; kind and considerate; determined and selfless. She is willing to learn new skills and is masterful in the way she protects those she loves. That is the person I met. No idea who this Charlotte Willet is."

She felt her energy drain away and she let her head rest on his shoulder as he sat beside her. "Simmons, you are too kind."

"I call it how I see it."

"I wish..."

"Yes...?"

"I wish I could disappear... with Edwin forever."

"Oh. Well. Then it is a good thing that you never intended to marry Dempsey. If you have truly given your heart to this Edwin, it is my hope he will prove more worthy of every expectation that you have of him. I trust he will be one who will protect and cherish your generous heart. You deserve no less, Little Martha."

She sat up and squeezed his arm. "Thank you, Simmons. Thank you." She leant in and quickly kissed his cheek. She stood up comforted, went over to the bowl and poured water from the kettle to lather up the suds.

6.

The mountain of dirty dishes from that meal piled higher and higher. Perhaps the task seemed more onerous tonight because Martha had lifted the veil on her background. Confessing to Simmons that dishwashing was never one of her responsibilities, made it somehow more unreasonable that tonight she here doing just that. But she persisted through the stacks anyway and was frustrated by the never-ending towers of dirty dishes that kept appearing on the bench beside her. With this special dinner on top of the standard catering for the inn-travellers, it seemed like it would never end.

Simmons watched her impatiently throw another wet towel onto the pile in the basket by the door and pick up another one. He came over to her. "You are going at this all wrong. Dishes are not just dishes... they are an opportunity."

She frowned at him in disgust. "You are mocking me! The only change they have succumbed to, are that the plates, and bowls, and saucers on this side are now spotless."

His sober face did not change. "I am completely serious. If you are just washing dishes, I would also struggle to climb such a mountain of tedium. But instead... a repetitive occupation like this, is an opportunity to escape... to go someplace else... to explore... to investigate."

"Impossible! I am chained to this bench. I am in a work gang, and you are the overseer with a slave-driver's lash."

"That is one way to look at it. You are obliged to do it whether you consider it that way or another. Or... I could be the ticket master who gives you passage to travel wherever you will. Would you not, at this very moment... prefer to be exploring exotic places... on the arm of your Edwin?"

"Edwin... is he here?" Her eyes leapt as she turned to look at the door. "I can go?"

Simmons swallowed and shook his head as he watched her eyes light up. "Grief. No! And I wouldn't tell you even if I thought he was – there are dishes to be done!"

"But you said..."

"I meant... why not use these dishes like cogs in those infamous time machines. Take yourself on a journey... transport yourself to him."

"How? I am here... in an apron, cleaning up this mess... such a lot of mess!"

"For someone who is intelligent, Little Martha, you are being quite tedious. That is not the dishes' fault. What would Edwin be doing at this moment?"

"This late in the evening? He would be working on the orders that he received during the day. He is a tailor, so he would be measuring and cutting and tacking suits."

"Tailor, huh?" Simmons looked at her curiously. *Definitely no pedigree hound.* "Have you ever been to his shop?"

"Oh yes... it is on Victoria Street. I would go there to check on Father's orders. It has a wonderful shopfront with an exquisitely tiled mosaic step; such elegant swirling script on the window..." She had paused; the plate in her hand sat half immersed in water.

"That's the idea. So, as you wash that plate, picture that window. Notice the light glinting on the glass, highlighting the writing. What does it say?"

"E. W. Couture. Fine Taylor. Custom-made suits. Made to measure. Distinguished furnishings for men."

"See your plate is clean. Take the next one and walk inside the shop. What do you notice?"

"There is dark wood panelling around the walls and a tidy orderliness to everything. The bolts of suiting fabric are arranged on the shelves according to tone. Tweeds. Wool. Serge. Twill. And the smell... it has the smell of refinement. Distinguished."

"Take the next bowl... and where is your man... Edwin... in this distinguished setting?"

"He is standing by the cutting table laying out a suit. There is the sharp sound of the fabric shears as he cuts the fabric. And there's a tailor's dummy standing beside him where he is tacking the lining..."

"You are in danger of rubbing the pattern off the china. Take the next plate."

"Now he is sitting cross-legged on the table in the manner of master tailors... stitching the seams so meticulously."

"See how you have gone through your pile? I was not mocking you, Little Martha. It is an opportunity..."

"That is quite ingenious, Simmons! Thank you." He turned away as he was shut out. Martha had gone back to her time-machine and into the arms of the one whom she loved.

⁂

After the lights had gone out in the main house, Simmons sat down, and Martha did a final wipe of the benchtop. He had taken two glasses from the shelf and a bottle of wine that had been recorked from the meal. He brought out two pieces of cake... layered Pumpkin, Ginger, Date and Treacle Stack Cake. He placed a slice before her on one of the fine china cake plates. "We are entitled to a treat, I think. We have conquered a rather remarkable evening."

"You saved a slice for us? With some wine?"

"The guests have gone to their beds satisfied; the kitchen has reverted to its quiet lull after being the hub of frantic industry all evening. It is appropriate that we take a moment to celebrate tonight's success."

She offered a tired nod, barely able to raise a smile. "I will confess that I have been curious about this cake. It has been given some stunning compliments. One would almost think that by the time you get to dessert, after such an array of excellent courses... you could let your guard down. But you don't. You take pride in your work, Cook Simmons... right to the end."

He shrugged. "There is a story where Jesus did a miracle of turning water into wine, after the hosts ran out of supplies. What he provided was the best wine those wedding guests ever experienced. He didn't do a shoddy job, just because the guests were full and past caring. He cared... and took pride to the last drop. I take my cue from the Master."

"Well, it is impossible to argue with that. You have obviously thought about this."

"I have. Excellence is a moral stamp, regardless of occupation. And I enjoy creating desserts, so I take the opportunity when I can. Desserts are none too appreciated around droving camps or shearing sheds... so this is as much a treat for me as those invited to Mrs Bailey's dinner party."

She took her cake fork and broke off a corner of the cake layers. Martha nibbled it thoughtfully and her face melted with delight. "Oh

Simmons, this is divine! So rich!" She paused again and savoured the moment with her eyes closed. "Hmmm... delicious!" She swirled her wine glass and took a sip. She took another taste of cake. "Oh! Somehow, this tastes like coming home."

Simmons nodded with approval and helped himself to his piece. He noted that she really was familiar with the finer things. The sliver cutlery, the fine china and crystal goblets were as usual for her, as an enamel pannikin was for him. She didn't faulter. It added weight to her story. He wondered who the real Martha was. Was this new story, another mask for her to stay in deep hiding? He was not certain.

She paused and pushed her plate away. She waved her cake fork over the sweet stack construction like a regal sceptre. "The clumsy name, that lists its ingredients like a recipe, that does not do this creation justice. It should be called something memorable... artistic... quirky... like... umm... *Treacle Homestead Baklava*. Or maybe just *Homestead Baklava*. It echoes of the layered classic Turkish sweet."

He looked at her with a raised brow. "You know your cuisine Little Martha. You show exceptional diversity in your tastes."

She shrugged. "Themed parties are quite the rage. Dressing up in an Ottoman kaftan with a filmy veil is quite flattering. It is inevitable such an event goes with flatbread, Turkish-Delight and Baklava."

"So, you have an international palate. I wonder what you think about Aussie cuisine. There is every potential for it to be as full-flavoured and as exciting as the most exotic destinations." He pushed the cake plate back in front of her.

She smiled and took another mouthful. "This has an echo of those exotic flavours... but it also feels uniquely Australian, straight off a sheep station. Is this a tribute to your mother? You reference her a lot in your cooking."

"Well...yes, in a way, it is. She was a master of pumpkin cakes and date loaves... so the pumpkin ginger cake interspersed with the layers of minced date filling is inspired by her idea of a decent morning tea."

"Decent?" She laughed as she took another sip of her wine. "I would say your creation here has outshone ordinary. Has she seen this? Does she approve?"

He shrugged as he swirled his glass. "Perhaps... she might have. She was also a practical, no fuss woman, so the layering would seem unnecessary bother for her. She was more a straight-down-the-line standard sort of cook. Culinary adventuring was not her style."

"Ah-huh! I knew it! You were raised in a kitchen! That is why this is so comfortable for you! Your apprenticeship started when you were toddling over flagstone floors, banging on pots and baking pans with wooden spoons. Cleavers and chopping boards were probably your baby toys. I bet you were teething on a knife steel. This is indeed the native habitat where you grew up."

He grinned. "You have given yourself a bit creative license there, Little Martha."

"Says the man who showed me how to climb mountains by walking into the imaginative halls of the fabled mountain king. You opened the door on imagination, so I think it is allowed. Is this how you survive the drudgery of cooking oatmeal porridge and ox-tail stews? I've wondered how you do it."

He shrugged. "I learnt early that mundane pays the bills. Creative keeps it interesting."

"Hmm. No doubt, another lesson from your mother... the plain-main cook." Martha took another forkful of cake and raised her glass. "Well, in honour of your mother... who taught you mastery with your artist's brushes and palette... she has done the next generation proud."

⁂

7

True to her prediction, Cyrus left in the morning with a group heading off to the goldfields. Martha watched him mount up, carefully hiding from behind a curtain. But it was not until his horse disappeared down the track, that she turned away from the window. She sighed, relieved, and felt a weight lift from her shoulders. She nodded to Simmons. "He is gone. I am safe for now."

"Surely you don't have to marry him, if your heart is set on another."

"Oh, I won't marry him. I told my father that if he insisted, I would disappear and disinherit, rather than marry outside my personal preference. My father didn't take me seriously then. But now that I have gone off the map, he is forced to offer a level of respect to my declaration. I will certainly not attach myself to one so determined to dismiss or misuse me."

Simmons nodded. He had no doubt that her Father was learning more about his daughter's capacity to be heard. Simmons was certainly learning that.

Another afternoon as she was cleaning the pans from the lunchtime cook, she took a deep breath and spoke very firmly. "I've thought about what you said, Simmons. Two months is not that tardy given that we will spend a lifetime together."

"So, you will not excuse Dempsey-the-philanderer? But Edwin-the-bitsa-hound gets a full reprieve for his careless and half-hearted behaviour? Given that he is the one who is courting above his station, I would have expected he would choose to be *more* attentive in courting civilities. It is a matter of grave presumption the way he is expecting you to stand around waiting for him to gather his manners."

"Come, Simmons, you agreed that he was more worthy of my affections than Cyrus."

"I said I was *hoping* that was the case, since you are so generous and lavish in your affection. It does not give him any entitlement to be overconfident as the privileged recipient of your regard. My mind is definitely not convinced either way. Like I said: tardy."

"You cannot be so inflexible! Surely you of all people know that there are practical matters to be taken into consideration. Love can surmount the grind of routines and survive any delay that circumstances might incur, given the right nurture and temperature of feeling."

"Humph. I hardly think neglect is the temperature or language of devotion. The man is probably hedging his bets."

"Why would you say that?"

"Because you said you had an agreement. It is now nearly *four* months since you sought refuge on my hearth. Twice what you spoke of. Have you heard from him at all?"

"We correspond of course. You are trying to dissuade me. But I will not be moved. I am sure there is a very reasonable explanation why he is taking so long."

"Well, it does show I was right about one thing..."

"What is that?"

"That you have a loyal heart, Little Martha. I have seen you as you really are. I met the person without the mask... the authentic you."

"And what is that like... seeing me as I am? Do you find that person dull and dense like most others?" She laughed lightly but watched him curiously out of the corner of her eye as she focused on the pan in her hand.

"Dull and dense?" he frowned with a shake of his head. "How could I think that? I suspect the Martha I have met is brighter and more sensational than Charlotte Willett could ever be... even in an expensive society gown. And determined! Not even mountains of kitchen dishes, or the need to wait tables like a commoner, will divert you. I believe that stacks evidence towards at least one quality that surprises me: nothing will move you once you have given your resolve to a course."

"Pfft! I never took you for an elitist, Simmons. You would do the same for someone you loved, if that was what was needed. I think we are more alike than you are inclined to give credit to."

"I doubt you have any evidence to support such a claim. When have I ever crossed the social divide so resolutely to claim the heart of someone I love?"

"Ahh... but I do see that. I see the loyally you ply to your craft through the mundane, because you love her... because you know the moments that you can truly spend together, the moments of creative synergy, the moments of intimate sharing, are worth all the time that you are apart, separated by the ordinary practical routine matters of life. You go through the motions of daily damper and mutton stew... because that is your ticket to crossing the social chasm to create extraordinary artistic moments like a Homestead Baklava." Martha grinned. She knew by the look on his face that she had shaved so very close to the truth. "I am right about this. You have a loyal heart too, Seth Simmons. With a great capacity for love."

Simmons sat silently. Hardly able to draw a breath. Finally, he spoke quietly. "Well, Little Martha, your assessment still needs to be tested. I am yet to declare any great love."

"Oh, your time will come. You will find your Edwin."

He pulled a dish from the oven and put it on a trivet. "I am definitely sure of one thing: I am not looking for Edwin," he said as he picked up a spoon and handed it to her, indicating for her to taste it.

She wiped her hands on a towel and took the spoon. She blew on it, waiting for it to cool and tasted it. "Oh... nice! Really nice. See. This is what I am talking about: a moment of love!" She tasted it again with a laugh. "Even if you are not going to confess your great love, I will do it for you. This is your moment... a moment worth waiting for!"

Simmons almost took her at her word... but before he could form the words, Amelia appeared at the door. "Excuse me, Simmons. There is a gentleman who has requested a private audience with... a Miss Willett."

Her heart leapt. "He's here? Did he give his name?"

Amelia looked at the card in her hand. "He did. Yes. Mr Edwin Couture."

Martha jumped up with a squeal! She bounced around the benches. "He's here! Finally, he is here!" She flashed a look at Simmons who stood leaning on the bench, his face unreadable. "See I was right! He has come. The accusation of tardy has been lifted."

"Only by you. It is still four months."

She took off her apron and bundled it up in a ball and threw it at him. It hit him in the head and landed in the dish on the bench with a plop. Martha flew passed Amelia, who raised her brow and called out, "He's waiting in the private drawing room..."

Simmons frowned and picked her apron up out of the dish. He stood up, and he threw it furiously into the basket by the door, full of used tea towels and aprons and wash cloths, waiting to be collected by the laundry maids.

Martha barely paused outside the drawing room door to smooth her skirt and pat her hair that refused to stay even. She opened the door and entered with the eagerness. Edwin turned and uncreased the frown on his brow, as she came quickly to embrace him. His suit was well cut and stylish. The hat in his hand was expensive. It defied all logic, that her father, who was a devotee of appearances, refused to appreciate how this man's handsome looks gave him a very striking manner. If she had not met him in amongst the trappings of a tailor shop, she expected he would be the object of envy in any gentlemen's club. She had told him so many times. He held her back at arm's length and looked her up and down with a suave smile on his lips.

"Charlotte. See. I told you I would come."

She dropped her arms and turned away. "You told me *two* months. And here it is *four*. Why have you kept me waiting so? I have been so anxious that you have forgotten me." Well... part of that was true. The bit about the time frame. Why would she defend him to Simmons and yet accuse him herself without hesitation? She frowned slightly at the other idea. She had not been sick with worry. Not in the slightest. She smoothed her brow and smiled. It had to be because Simmons was right. She was loyal; she had an unshakeable confidence of Edwin's love. Even when delayed, an enduring love could wait.

Edwin cleared his throat and rubbed his temple restlessly. "There were problems with the shop. I have been organising the sale, and there were deferments with the transfers. But it is all settled now, and it is good to have that out of the way. So, be reassured Charlotte, once we are married, we will not have to worry about the menial matters of trade."

"What do you mean? I had no idea you were intending to sell your shop. Surely you are going to keep it! It was your father's. You told me that you appreciated how you could take an ordinary man and make him distinguished. Provide your patrons with the air of confidence. That the cut of a suit was just one mark of..."

He cut her off impatiently. "You would tie me to trade just like my family? Charlotte! I expected more from your regard. We spoke about the freedom it would bring, to be part of something that was classless. My Forefathers fought for this ideal."

"I am pretty sure, that what we spoke about, did not mean you merely expected to join the ranks of society. I thought the revolution was against those elite excesses."

"Charlotte? Why would you say that? We love each other. For us to be together, it is right that we have the same social opportunities. With you by my side, I can mingle in the right circles. The husband of a Willett needs the prestige you deserve. Membership to certain gentlemen clubs offer that. This is the way I will win your family over." Edwin stared at her, his handsome chin tilted at just the right angle to look distinguished and noble. "After all... I have won your heart, haven't I?"

Her mind went blank. Was this all it had been about? Had he captured her heart so he could access an exclusive pass into this colonial pseudo-nobility? Australian Sterling, it was called. Even if that was his expectation, she still didn't think he would be given that privilege. People didn't move up... only down. And she had been prepared for down. After a long pause, she shook her head, and smiled, and ruffled her short-cropped hair with her fingers.

He focused and gasped, as if seeing her for the first time since she had come into the room. "What have you done to your hair?"

She shrugged nonchalantly and then smiled at him enchantingly. "I did it for us. I had it cut it off, so, no one would recognise me. Specifically, certain people from home came here, searching me out... to take me back to marry another."

"Dempsey?"

She nodded.

Edwin stared at her up and down, as if he had trouble hearing her words. Finally, his lip curled. "I would not be surprised if he saw you. In fact – he probably did. It is obvious why Dempsey would not acknowledge you. It is indecent for a lady to be looking like that!" He gasped again as he focused on her attire. "And what you are wearing? Why would you do this?"

"It is all part of our plan... my ruse to escape being exposed. I did it so we could be together!" She stepped towards him and wondered if he would really understand that working as a maid, or even cutting her hair, was no sacrifice at all.

Edwin took a step back. "Scripture clearly says it is a disgrace for a woman to cut her hair. You are shorn like a sheep. We can't be married while you are looking like that!"

"Then we wait until it grows. I have been waiting for you. Now it is your turn, Edwin. Our love is strong." She looked up at him, entreating him to understand.

Disgust burned in his eyes. Perhaps that look carried the revelation which seared over her feelings. She swallowed and took a breath. Her voice was calm. Her tone measured. "So... let me get this straight. You came here to collect me... like something from a catalogue, only to find that I don't look like what you expect, and you want a refund? What will you say when I tell you that I have been working as a scullery maid, making my way, waiting tables, and washing dishes?"

"That is ridiculous. Of course, you wouldn't. A lady doesn't do that."

"This one did!"

He stopped and frowned, as if what she said finally registered. "Charlotte, why would you need to *make your way?*"

She took a deep breath... and spoke it out, quiet and restrained. "I told Father I am in love. That I would disregard my income rather than marry without you. He does not approve of your trade, Edwin. I had to disinherit for us to be together."

"You did what? Why on earth would you do that? Oh, Charlotte – that is crazy talk! If you truly loved me, you would find a way for us to marry properly. Surely if you went back to your father... confess it as a moment of weakness, that he would reconsider."

"Signed it in blood. There is no going back."

"I cannot believe that after all that I have done, that you would betray me like this! I have waded through treacherous marshes of social disregard. I have climbed endless mountains; forded uncharted rivers... all in the name of my love for you."

She laughed at his melodrama; mirthless and pained. She had literally done all of those things for months, and he had no interest in finding out what her endeavours had been. "Well, I guess you now can see what your devotion has bought you: a penniless woman with cropped hair, who has learnt to wash dishes."

"If I wanted a woman with those credentials, there are plenty of handsomer women who would be willing to marry me. Careful Charlotte, or you will find yourself alone, enjoying a lifetime of squalor, if you don't take a more sensible approach to this situation. You should go back to your father. He is devoted to you. Even now, he would change is mind."

She shook her head. And her frizzy hair flopped in her eyes. She swiped at it roughly. Whatever she knew about her relationship with her father was now no longer his business. Not now. "Oh no, he was most definite, Edwin. Most definite! He said that if I wanted to marry a trade then I would need to slog like the working class myself."

Edwin turned away and stared out the window and watched worn-out miners who were leaving their dreams of gold, moving on to the next published declaration of where a strike was to be made. He turned back to her and adjusted the lapels of his suit jacket. "You know we cannot marry now. It is impossible."

She noticed the handsome tilt to his chin as if in some way this travesty was all her fault, and *he* was disappointed in *her*. Not heartbroken though. There was no sign of a broken heart. She noticed that. "I think I do realise this," she said as she shook her head and squeezed her eyes shut. Was she hoping her sense of humiliation would hide in the dark behind her closed lids long enough for her to find some privacy? She paused a moment and wondered what she wanted from him. Some sort of apology for her wounded feeling? Or a revelation that love is stronger than a society club membership? But there was nothing he would offer. His eyes had iced over, but the cover on her heart had not closed over well enough to repel the barbs of injury that his disgust shot through her. She turned and ran. She had no idea of anything else in that moment. She just wanted to yell and kick and scream and be that four-year-old again. Who wants to be a grown-up when it hurts so much?

⁂

8.

Amelia knocked on the door to the domestics' quarters. "Excuse me girls. Just allow me a quiet moment with Martha." The other staff nodded and left. Amelia sat down on Martha's bunk and cleared her throat uncertainly.

Martha sat up. She had never set foot in such humble quarters until she was required to sleep here. Why would Amelia check on her in a place like this? "Ma'am... you didn't have to come here. It must be strange for you to be sitting on a servant's bed."

"Tsk! I have spent plenty a night sleeping in beds worse than this. It is a familiar space."

"Oh. I... I didn't realise." Well, it was not familiar to her. But it had served a purpose and that had made it tolerable. Now that purpose was gone. Edwin was gone.

"I came to see if you were okay. Simmons said that you didn't come back to the kitchen."

"I... Oh... I guess that means I am let go."

"Do you want to be let go?" Amelia paused and compassion filled her eyes. "Don't be mad at Simmons, but he told me that Martha is not your real name. That you are Miss Willett. That Mr Couture was using your real name... not the made-up one. I misunderstood. I took it to be the other way 'round."

Simmons trusted this lady. That was a reference she could respect. She was, after all, sitting on a servant's bunk showing concern to one of her working maids. "Simmons is right. My name is Charlotte Willett. Yes... those Willetts. Cyrus Dempsey... he came to your birthday dinner... I disappeared to escape an inopportune marriage to him. I was meeting up with Edwin here. I intended to marry him instead."

"Oh! What an adventure! You must love this Edwin very much." Amelia had not even blinked. No gasps of shock from the shadows of scandal.

"More like a misadventure. I was seduced by Edwin's good looks. Something Simmons had said made me doubt, I guess. So, I tested the nature of his devotion. But without the money, Edwin's love was also gone. So quickly gone. I hardly know what to do now. I believed in him so wholeheartedly. I believed in us. I feel like I just want to disappear again."

"Oh Martha, you must be so very sad. I am sorry we cannot do more to help you."

"Being a scullery-maid with not a care in the world has been a wonderful escape. But life here was a mask. A pretend. I think it is time to go back."

"Go back? Where?"

"Back home; it is my destiny it seems. I came here to meet my Love... and see how badly that has ended. So, I will go home and perhaps allow my wounded heart to heal."

"Oh..." Amelia paused for a long while. "You could stay a while longer... take some time to recover. We would not expose you. Staying here would not be just for you... we appreciate your help as well."

"Oh, thank you, Amelia. Your offer is generous, but I think I will go. I have enjoyed wearing a Redwood apron... but I know this is over now. I am resolved that from now on, love will have to search me out and find me. Amelia, I hope you easily find someone to help

Simmons. The traffic from the goldfields is fast running down, so perhaps hiring may be less difficult now."

"Well, you stay as long as you need. Or go back to your family if that suits you better. But, Martha do it with your head held high. You chose something bold and adventurous to explore where this road might take you... and you saw and learnt shiny new things... even if it was not as you expected. And in spite of what you insist, I don't think it was all pretend."

"Oh Amelia, sometimes you say the most profound things..."

"Pfft. I know I am not clever... not in the way that Bailey is clever, managing this place... or Simmons is clever, cooking food fit for a palace... but I see with my heart. That is as good as clever. That is something my clever Bailey taught me."

"Well, I met you... and your family... and Simmons. They have been my shining new things I found travelling this road. You are right. I am glad our paths have crossed. That has not been wasted. I have done things I never thought possible. My family will never understand, and I know this is something that I can never share with them, but I will hold it dear... close to my heart, forever."

⁂

9.

Mr Willett sat at the breakfast table trying to read his newspaper. He was unsettled and he sighed heavily, folded the paper, and put it to the side. He placed his eyeglasses in the ceramic dish placed at his elbow for that purpose and indicated for another hot cup of tea to be poured. "Ask Mary to come," he said as he sighed again and distractedly drank his tea.

"Yes, Sir?"

"Mary... Mary..."

"Yes, Sir?"

"How long have you been in service with us?"

"Nigh twenty-four years sir. Mrs Willett, God rest her soul, appointed me when she was expecting our lovely Charlotte."

"Yes. Yes. And it seems that for someone so trusted that it would be a shame for you to need to find other employment. At your age it would be difficult to find another appointment."

"Oh Sir! I told you I do not know what has happened! She has not confided in me at all Sir. Please..."

"Oh come, come. Mary I am not to be trifled with any longer. I know that nursery maids, turned personal attendants, are trusted confidants. You *must* be privy to what happened! She has been home now for over three weeks... and not a word. Not a word about anything! She refuses to see Mr Dempsey. She refuses to take her food in the dining room when we have company. She refuses to accept any invitations. She refuses everything! Are you the one who is encouraging this uncharacteristic wilfulness? Because if that is the case you can no longer stay in our employ. I think that enough is enough!"

Charlotte stood calmly at the door in her tea dress. "I have not refused you, Father. It is not fair that you fly out these accusations against Mary. I have told you over and over that Mary was not privy to my plans. And I have told you... on a daily basis, that I want to take some time to reflect on what I intend to do from here. The truth is that being away has changed me, and I need to search out this meaning for myself."

"The truth? How can I possibly know what is the truth, Charlotte? I know you are changed, but I am quite at a loss to know what to do now. Dr Phillips was brought in to see if you were recovering satisfactorily."

"And Father, did he not reassure you that I am quite well? He said I needed to take a little rest. Well, this is me following his advice. Taking rest. Doctor's orders."

"I think this is enough rest. Quite enough. It is time you resumed life. I am bombarded by requests and inquiries on every side for your attention. What am I to say to them?"

"Oh, Father. This is not beyond you. Tell them what you told them while I was away." She sat at the table and nodded to Mary who automatically filled her cup with tea and brought her toast from the sideboard. "Thank you, Mary... no need to fuss," she said gently.

Her father stared at her with a frown. "I told them that you had gone to Venice. You have spoken wistfully about Venice a number of times. How else could I explain such an extended absence outside of the marvel of exotic travel?"

"Venice? Ingenious. See? I was quite correct. It was not beyond you. Although the time frames to get there and back, are less than accurate."

"I certainly would not tell them that we thought you had gone to the Goldfields. But it is evident that you were not there either. Inspector Saunders from the Peace Regiment heard nothing the entire time you were gone."

"Father, I have reassured you over and over: I did not go to the Goldfields."

"Then where were you?"

She sighed. She had to give him something. "I was at a beautiful retreat... close to the mountains. I spent a lot of time reflecting and praying..." That was what it was like for her. When she wrote to Amelia, and reassured her that she had arrived home safely, she described her time there had been like lodging at Redwood Retreat. It was fitting.

Mr Willett gasped. "Oh Charlotte, Charlotte... are you considering becoming a postulant in a religious sense? Tell me this is not true!"

She stared at him for a moment. A nun living in a cloister. Taking orders? Living a life close to God? Charlotte liked the way Simmons talked about following the example of Jesus. Not complicated, yet endlessly inspiring and challenging. Yet, as comforting a sheltered religious life would be, it would just be another mask. "No, Father. I don't think being a nun is the only way to live a life close to God. I know people who live very spiritual lives without donning a habit." Like Simmons for example. He spoke of God in the most genuine way. Following the master. Living a life of excellence. Doing well wherever he was.

"Then tell me, Charlotte. What am I to do? Mr Dempsey has all but given up."

"One thing you could do, Father, is to encourage Mr Dempsey to give up entirely. We were never engaged... and we will never *be* engaged. It is unkind to suggest to him that I may change my mind, because I will not. There is absolutely no hope of that happening at all. If you try to force my hand, I will simply disappear again. Perhaps this time I may not return so promptly." That was plain enough. But then, she had said it plainly before.

Mr Willett gasped again. "This was about your engagement to Cyrus Dempsey? Why didn't you say so?"

"I *have* said so... many times." She turned to spread some plum fruit preserve on her toast and thought about pitting plums for roast duck. Simmons was everywhere. Still. How could that be? What was that about?

"Well... okay, okay." He shook his head. "Have you really broken Mr Dempsey's heart? You do get away with such unconventional ways."

"I doubt his heart is broken, Father. Every time I hear of Cyrus, he is on the arm of another lady. He will be fine."

"Well! That is outrageous behaviour! So soon after terminating a betrothal."

"I know, Father. Shameless. Even though I will remind you that we were never actually engaged."

"It is just that the list of eligible suitors is so short. Cyrus seemed like a hopeful option in so many ways. Are you sure?

"I am sure."

"Many of the young men who come knocking are so unsuitable. Up to now I have been telling them you were spoken for."

"I am okay if you continue to do so."

"But, Charlotte, Charlotte, I don't want you ending up an old maid. You are already past your year of majority."

"It wouldn't be so terrible. My life here with you is satisfactory. Oh, Father. there is no need to worry. But if you must, distract them."

"Distract them? Your mother used to say the perfect distraction was hosting a ball. We could hold a ball I suppose. Hmm. A ball would be a suitable distraction."

"Oh, I don't know, Father, that seems like a lot of bother."

"No, no. Hosting a ball could indeed be the perfect distraction. We could do it in the name of your coming home, and in service of your mother's charities. What about a Masquerade in the spirit of Venice? It is evident you didn't actually get there, so I will bring Venice to you. This is exactly the way to offer distraction to those restless eligible members of society." His eyes lit up like he had been given a prize stallion with impeccable bloodlines. "Yes, Charlotte. Charlotte! This is a wonderful idea! Yes! Yes, we will do that. We will not wait. In two weeks."

"Two weeks? Father, I don't think even Mrs Jensen can manage something like that in two weeks!"

"No, I am decided. There is absolutely nothing to be gained by dallying around the idea." And he stood up excitedly. His boredom had evaporated. His anxiety about her unwillingness to disclose where she had been, had dissolved; his worry over her spinster status had dissipated. His hope soared as he imagined all the potential suitors this would draw to his honeypot. "I will call on Mrs Jensen immediately so she can organise everything. You won't have to do a thing, except choose your gown, and your mask. Oh, this is a very good idea!" He now had a project to focus on. Charlotte was already sorry for Mrs Jensen, yet relieved that a suitable decoy from her father's relentless interrogations had been found. For the next two weeks she would be more or less left alone. She could sort a gown and a matching mask in her sleep.

❧

10

Charlotte scanned the ball room. The music swelled and the dancers twirled. The array of colours was glorious; the masks worn by the guests were ornate; the chamber music – stirring; the decorations in the room – opulent. Mrs Jensen had done an accomplished job, even with the impulsive timeframe. But then, her father had spared no expense, so this was no surprise. Charlotte was thankful for the inspiration that had overtaken her father to suggest a masquerade ball. In the five weeks since coming home, Charlotte's hair had grown some... but not sufficiently to tame it, at least not in the way she was accustomed. No amount of beating it down could achieve that strict smoothness she was familiar with. She had taken her lopped braid to the wigmaker and a braided piece had been created for her to wear in public. Charlotte liked the idea actually. It saved sitting for hours, having her hair braided. She adjusted her gloves and moved the lace mask, bejewelled with diamantes, over her eyes. Her gown elegantly flowed around her in rich ripples of burgundy.

The list of invitations was modest but exclusive, and those wanting to win an audience with Charlotte on the dance floor would have to first find their way through any number of other masked dancers. One evening in a dance hall – she could tolerate that, if this was the price she had to pay for a fortnight of peace. It was worth it.

"Ma'am..." A rich smooth voice captured her attention and she turned and smiled into the mask of a tall gentleman with dark hair.

She curtsied. "Good evening, Sir."

"May I have this dance?"

She titled her head. "No fancy introductions? No social chit-chat? You get straight to the point, Sir."

"I would think the point of a Ball is to dance. And I think the point of a Masquerade, is to avoid the social courtesies of having to be benignly amusing." He held out his gloved hand.

She nodded and smiled and took his lead. "It is a valid argument you make. So yes... it would be my pleasure."

"You are very trusting, Ma'am. I could be anyone... leading you into this swirling morass of masked dancers."

"Oh. I am confident enough of the etiquettes required to be partakers of these exclusive events. Mrs Jensen is renowned in organising strictly monitored guest lists. It would take ingenuity and audacity beyond most people, to surmount the mountains of protocols to get in here uninvited. And on top of all that... there is the price tag required to support my mother's legacy of charities. I doubt anyone would go to all that bother if their intentions were not honourable."

"They might pay that price, and go to all that effort, if it meant they could secure a dance with yourself. Perhaps someone would traverse the social divide for that privilege. It would be incentive enough for me," he confessed as he twirled her around and back into his arms.

She laughed. "Charming. You might not lead with benign social courtesies, but you are a master of flattery and compliments none the less."

"Only when the object of those compliments are worthy recipients. Your gown this evening flatters you in every way. It is sensational; the rich colour of claret... like the perfect accompaniment to a fine dessert."

She was amused and laughed. "I don't think I have ever been told I look like pudding before. You may have spoilt your perfect record of pleasing compliments with that comment, Sir."

He did not pause, but confidently led, moving among the other couples without hesitation. "I don't think my record suffers, for a fine wine is an essential accompaniment to any rich dining fare. Tonight, I feast."

She shook her head, and chuckled, and she felt some of her hair falling loose from under her braided hairpiece, as they dipped and twirled while they danced. When the music slowed, he gently tucked that whisp of hair behind her ear and adjusted her mask. "Careful M'lady, your mask is slipping. It would not do to have me see who you really are."

"You need not fear. I am the mistress of my mask. I have learnt to be careful. I do not allow just anyone to see who is behind my mask."

"Intriguing," he murmured looking down at her, as the music stopped, and they stepped back and bowed. "Aristocracy... it is the perfect disguise, is it not? It is, indeed, an effective mask for all sorts of occasions, don't you think, Little Martha?" He said it with a bow and then turned and melted into the crowd of dancers on the floor.

She gasped. "Simmons!" She looked to where he had gone, but he had vanished. She went to follow, but she was hemmed in. Someone accosted her for the next dance. By the time she sought out the serving staff and found her way to the kitchen, she created a lot of confusion. No one had heard or seen any one by the name of Seth Simmons. She spent the rest of the evening looking for the tall dancer with the dark hair and the perfect disguise.

As she was going upstairs to her room, one of the maids came to her and handed her a mask. It was identical to the one worn by her tall, masked dance partner. She picked it up and turned it over. Inside, was written a message in a scrolled hand...

The lines of poetry inside the mask ran through her mind, over and over, like an unsolvable riddle. It tormented her with its meaning. Her father often commented on her distractibility, and on a daily basis he urged her to become more focused. But that made no sense to Charlotte. Focused on what? She had no serious occupation that offered her any meaningful purpose. Some women tried to enlist her on their committees... but she declined... waiting for some incentive to captivate her attention. Distraction from the listlessness became her motivating mission. Mostly that involved walks in the park and reading books in the garden. Sometimes she even stole over to the East Wing, to the kitchen, to see how she might ply herself to industry there. But the staff would stare at her confused and stand to attention until she left.

Since the success of the exclusive masquerade ball, it was apparent that Charlotte was back on the social scene, so invitations from various circles started to pour in. Charlotte was aware these socials were not the happy occasions like the birthday party at Redwood Inn. In truth they were networking events, where everyone came with an agenda to push, or a cause to promote, and she was invited because her family had more money than most. Her father spoke seriously of her obligations of being a member of society, and she acknowledged that what he preached probably had an element of truth, but it did nothing to capture her imagination. It was an exhausting exercise, discerning those who had hidden intentions and those who didn't. Everyone, by default, became an object of suspicion. Edwin's misuse of her heart haunted her like a ghost. Simmons commended her judgement regarding Dempsey, but when it came to Edwin, she had failed to discern the truth completely. This awareness constantly nipped at her heels, cautioning her to not be naively taken-in again.

It was a relief to correspond with Amelia. Her simple language was like a breath of fresh air. The affection she held for her husband and devotion to her children was so unlike the incessant comparisons her social companions made. Charlotte wrote to Amelia about the masquerade ball and her absolute shock when she realised Simmons was her masked admirer. "How could that even be possible?" she wrote. "It is unthinkable that a man of his station secured admission to our ball without an invitation or patron. Since he wore gloves, I was deprived of sighting that identifying scar on his hand, which would remove any doubt. And he danced so masterfully! But if I am correct, and he somehow did cross that social divide... why would he disappear without acknowledgement of our encounter? The kitchen staff looked at me as if I was quite insane when I went to make an inquiry..." The mystery continued to tease her.

On another occasion, out of boredom, Charlotte wrote to Amelia about the tedious parade of pending invitations that arrived at her door. For example, the Ladies' Missionary League was hosting a fundraiser, themed in the Roman Empire. She was amused at how Mrs Jensen marketed the idea when she dropped off the invitation in person. Apparently, if the guests come as their favourite New Testament Biblical character, then the Clergy could not complain about the proliferation of togas or consider such a fundraising event was inappropriate. Its most commending feature was their unapologetic intent to extract as much money as possible from their patrons. That seemed a more honest agenda than most.

In her next letter, Amelia enthusiastically encouraged Charlotte to step outside her normal comforts and accept this invitation. Charlotte was not as animated by the idea as Amelia, but if nothing else, it would offer a topic to write about in her next letter. Charlotte didn't take long to decide from the list of suggestions offered by the Ladies' League, as to who her character would be. Martha. The friend of Jesus. The one who offered hospitality to Jesus on many occasions as he travelled through the village of Bethany. It was Martha who was misjudged and misunderstood, who acquired the undeserved disrepute for attending to practical matters, for being industrious while her sister sat down and enjoyed their visitor's company. Martha of Bethany grieved her brother's death, and Jesus came to breathe comfort into her grief, and life into her brother. Charlotte wished Jesus would do the same for her grief, even though no one had actually died.

Charlotte thought it was fitting that her middle name was Martina, which she understood was an exotic variation of Martha. Growing up, she shared a joke with her nursery maid, as she read this bible story to her, that they were just like family: Mary and Martha. That was where she pulled the inspiration for her pseudonym, the night she fled to Redwood Inn. Rather than feeling disconnected from the plainness of this character, she felt it fitted her well. Misjudged and misunderstood, she wistfully hoped that, like Martha, she could use practical matters to distract her. If there was any hope that she could get away with it, she even considered going back to the kitchen and demanding that she be allowed to do some washing up.

So, at Amelia's encouragement, she accepted the invitation to the costume party. Guests were required to nominate their chosen character on their written RSVP. Charlotte put together the ensemble of a humble Hebrew handmaiden and chose a coarse-weave apron in the manner of serving girls. She wore an eastern veil, and rather than having exotic jewels and pearls adorning her forehead, she chose humbler version of rustic wooden beads. She had fun putting the arrangement together, and although she would have loved to have her hair long, she thought her ornately braided hairpiece was less fitting than her short frizzy hair. Simmons had said this style suited her, and that offered more inspiration than an exotic braid. She was content that her humble attire suited her well enough.

And so, her anticipation for this evening increased, as part of her program of distraction. She was escorted to the venue by her father, who had gracefully declined the invitation himself to escape the frivolity of dressing up. He made a generous donation to the Ladies' League for the privilege of avoidance. From the moment Charlotte stepped from the carriage she become Martha again.

Some of these themed parties had a reputation of being pedantic in their pursuit of authentic details. This event was less strict, given that Mrs Jensen was working to a restrictive budget to maximise missionary funds. The music was the contemporary standard quartet; the decorations were missionary frugal; and the food, loosely Middle Eastern. Actually, as Martha inspected the tasters, she acknowledged the food was probably the most accurate detail of all. There were olives and figs and grapes and fish; some flatbread, creatively made into a Roman Pinza, which their hostesses assured her was an Italian form of cheese pie that dated back to the Roman Empire and was to be eaten with fingers for an authentic ethnic feel.

As each person handed in their ticket, they were given a packet with a name-badge in it. This became the basis of the introductory parlour game. While the music played, they were tasked with finding the character whose name they were given. It was fun. There were toga's aplenty; regal Roman emperors and empresses; imposing centurions and gladiators. There were disciples, tax-collectors, fishermen, lepers, and beggars. It was a wonderful mishmash of costume play. When Martha read the name of the guest she was to seek out, she smiled. Of course. Lazarus. How appropriate that she was to find her character's brother. So she went on her mission, mixing in amongst the guests. "I am Martha of Bethany, have you seen my brother, Lazarus?" And the play-acting continued as she was given condolences for her loss, all happily delivered, of course, in keeping with the festive cheerfulness of the occasion. And yet not one person offered a hint as to where he might be. Couples were beginning to find each other. Martha was becoming a little embarrassed that she could not find the character on the badge. It was about then that she saw him, standing beside an artificial ornamental date palm that occupied the corner, near the back exit. He was wrapped like a mummy... barely able to move, swaddled head to toe in burial cloths. "Hello. I am Martha... I am wondering if you are my brother, Lazarus?"

His eyes and mouth were visible, the wrapping of the bandages had at least given him that dispensation. He chuckled. "Yes, I am Lazarus," he said, and he paused as she pinned his name badge to his costume. "Would it be terribly ignorant if I gave you your badge to pin on yourself? Grave clothes are a terrible incumbrance. My apologies that I could not make any significant contribution to being found. I fear my entombment meant I've nearly missed the whole event."

She laughed at his plight, relieved that she had finally located her partner for the game. "Well, I am glad we have found each other, although we were far too late to secure a prize. Your efforts to stay in character are impressive. I was convinced there would be at least one couple here tonight who would not meet up."

"And yet... here we are. You would be surprised at some of the guesses people have offered to explain the nature of my predicament. An Egyptian mummy – with no consideration given to the obvious detail that we are here in Roman times. Another suggestion was that I am Herod's latest assassination victim... or even Jesus himself, embalmed and buried after the crucifixion. That aligns too closely to blasphemy for my liking."

"How did you even get here tonight? Your costume is a monumental hinderance to moving about."

"I found my place, and someone generously proceeded to embalm me. A little macabre, I thought, as far as costumes go, but far less taxing than the getup required for a Roman gladiator. A pair of white gloves and a sheet, and I was set."

"But hardly flattering. Wouldn't you have preferred to don the costume of a Roman Caesar or some other remarkable character? It seems unnecessary that you feel compelled to sacrifice your liberty to circulate, in loyalty to your character's entombment. Your devotion to the parameters set by the Ladies' League is unexpected."

"Caesar is a salad... and 'remarkable' is unnecessary if this costume affords me the opportunity for interesting conversation and fine company just as well as any other. No sacrifice at all, I would say."

"I am also wondering how you intend to eat tonight when you are all but completely encased."

"I will confess I was hoping to meet a serving girl... a Martha-type character who might be generous enough to ferry some options to my side. I really cannot walk in these bindings."

"Oh. So, you would you have *me* sacrifice my entire evening in service to you? That is an audacious expectation if ever there was one... brother Lazarus." But she wasn't offended. Just amused. He sounded like he didn't mind one way or another. And her curiosity, kindled by the bold request, was distracting.

"Of course, I would not see my sister's entire evening spoilt, but a drink would be appreciated. It is very warm plight being embalmed... not at all the deathly cold experience that is its reputation. Besides, I am not yet ready to face the typical array of obnoxious lobbyists trying to secure donations on the side. To canvas patrons for another cause is brazenly disrespectful of the Ladies' League's endeavours."

She laughed at his fun, but as she turned away to gather them both a chair, she was thoughtful. Even though he joked, they shared a common reluctance to start that political parade. She loosened some of Lazarus' wraps so he could sit. And then she secured them both a drink and placed the glass of punch in his gloved hands.

He nodded his thanks. "This is refreshing, thank you. So, tell me... why did you choose your character? I recognise you well enough, Miss Charlotte Willett... even behind your veil. Why wouldn't you also choose a costume that is fashionable and popular? You could carry the elegance of a Roman toga acceptably."

"Perhaps my name and family's reputation belie my ease with being out front and centre. Martha is famed for her background role. It could be, that like yourself, I am comfortable avoiding social banter and am amused to find the opportunity for interesting conversation without the price tag of a donation."

"Well in that case, you might be disappointed. I could be in need of funds. Since I am Lazarus, risen from the dead, you could help me set up a booth so people's curiosity of eternity could be appeased by plying me with questions to share my experiences of the here-after. Which I might do... for a fee. Or... I could be waiting to slather guilt all over your reputable social conscience, to secure your generous support of... something I am passionate about. What about the terrible neglect facing the crypts and memorials of community figures who have passed on? That is a social disgrace, and it would be fitting that I support their upkeep, since my character, Lazarus, spent four days in such a place."

She laughed. "If your intent was to extract funds from my father's chequebook, I suspect you would have already started your lobbying. Besides, you don't strike me as someone ruthlessly concerned with the ostentatious memorials of our forefathers."

"Am I so transparent? I was hoping these trappings would hide my lack of ambition."

"Well, it is not your lack of ambition that I notice, but your..." She paused, unwilling to voice to the sentiment that came to her mind. *Kindness.*

"Well, if lack of ambition is a flaw, I would not dare add to it by being inattentive. So, I will notice how you transform an ordinary serving girl's garb to a look of sublime elegance. Your modest ensemble is tasteful, and very flattering. You did well to avoid the toga after all."

She smiled and accepted the compliment. "Well since a serving girl's role is to serve, I will go and find ourselves a selection of Roman delicacies." She brought back the plates and curiously looked at the bound Lazarus. "You haven't told me your name. Surely that is unfair when you recognised me straight away."

"I think it is fitting that for this occasion, I am Lazarus, and you are Martha. The rest of our lives can remain unnoticed and unsolicited for just one evening surely."

She looked into his eyes and nodded appreciatively. They were brown. Kind. "The idea is a relief. I appreciate the kindness..." There. She said it. However, it did little to soothe her curiosity. "But isn't a significant part of the story of Lazarus, where Martha and her sister Mary were given the directive outside the tomb to unbind the risen Lazarus, so he could walk free? Sir, would you have me release you from your bindings of death so you can walk around... and perhaps eat more comfortably?" If she could see his face, she might recognise him. Something felt familiar in his manner.

"I agree that the make-believe is endearing, but if I allow you to unwrap me, I will be exposed, and no longer just Lazarus." He stared at the plate on a pillared occasional table and changed the subject. "Well, I must admit the food looks ordinary."

She laughed. "You sound just like my friend..." She gasped and stopped, and looked back at his eyes... but he had taken up some grapes and was turned away as he was navigating feeding them to himself with focused attention. "Simmons? Are you really Simmons?" she asked with a whisper.

"And who is this Simmons? Is he your friend?" he said flippantly, waving the grapes in his gloved hand.

"Oh yes! A wonderful friend..."

"Oh. Then already I am sorry I am just Lazarus and I wish I was him. I must sincerely apologise for detaining you from his wonderful company. You have ferried a stash of food to my side; so, you are released from any obligation to attend to your resurrected brother any further. If you have more interesting company to keep, why would you delay and stay with one wrapped up in tomb clothes?" He said it lightly, entertained by her look of mortification.

"Oh no... I did not mean you were a burden. My friend is not here... but..."

"You didn't invite him? Surely the Ladies' League would appreciate one more donation to their missionary cause."

"Well perhaps... but he doesn't live here. He lives in another world and our paths no longer cross. But I miss his good humour, and his predilection for wonderful food. He would agree with you, that the Roman menu is a little mundane, even if it holds to a level of authenticity."

"Well, the man has good taste. Proven, if he can claim you as his friend, and that his palate runs higher than these first-century pickings. Although... I am a little impressed with the Roman Pinza... that is quite a sensation. Try it... what do you think?" She took a nibble, and he shook his head. "No. No. Take a bite. Take a hearty serving-girl bite. Tell me what you think."

"Oh! That is unexpectedly tasty! Yes. I like that. I like that a lot."

His eyes went thoughtful. "Yes. I agree. Unexpected."

"Well, if you deny being Simmons, then I have no other recourse than to assume you are Lazarus. Although it does seem unfair... that you know my name, when I can't even see your face."

"Oh come... it is a mere detail. But tell me, did this Simmons desert you? Is that why you anticipated that I might be him?"

"No... no... it is complicated. I worked with him for a period. It was only a few months... but it seemed like a lifetime in other respects."

"A couple of months is transformed into a lifetime... that sounds excessively tedious. Was he working with you on one of your charity projects?"

"Sort of. He was supporting me in a particular endeavour. And I appreciated his help."

"I see... and now you miss him? Have you tried to contact him?"

"I want to... but..."

"But...?"

"Well, he thinks I am betrothed to another, and probably assumes I am married by now. The last time I saw him... I was going to be engaged."

"Ahh... and now the web of intrigue weaves tighter. This Simmons is exposed as an immoral fop, moving in on a lady already committed to another."

"No! That is unfair. He would never do that. Besides I didn't become engaged. I have wondered what Simmons would say if he knew that my heart longs to... talk with him?"

"Oh. Talk? That sounds... dull. And yet... Martha of Bethany, you are not a dreary conversationalist."

"Neither is he. I cannot explain it... but he knows me better than any other person I have ever met."

"Hmm..." he said thoughtfully. "All this is beginning to sound more serious than sociable conversation. I suspect he is revealed, not just as any casual friend... but as a... romantic interest? Does he know this?"

"Oh no! That would be unseemly. Yet the truth is that you are probably right. I think it is more. I have wondered if I am actually in love with him. I think about him all the time... but I have no way of contacting him."

"Don't you know where he lives?"

"Well, I did... obviously. I correspond with a mutual friend... but she hardly mentions him at all... mostly she relates stories about her children, which I do enjoy. But it means I don't know if he is still there or whether he has moved on."

"This other man... the one you were engaged to... the gossip columns have not mentioned that... which is an uncharacteristically benevolent oversight on their part. What happened to him?"

"Our understanding was secret and informal. I thought I would be blissfully married by now, but the attachment ended abruptly. It turns out that he was less in love with me, and more besotted with my income. It was a hard blow to come to terms with. Attending these events, this is my attempt to start to put back together the pieces of my broken heart. So, being allowed to sit here in the corner, away from the demanding scrutiny of gilded society, with a swaddled corpse is quite a relief. Thank you, Lazarus, for being the means of my escape."

Lazarus went quiet.

"No witty quip in response to my foolish infatuation or the tragic state of my heart?"

"I... no... I have nothing. I am embarrassed that someone, who would call himself a gentleman, could so sorely misuse you. Even if he was flexing his muscles to gain access to the traditional entitlements needed to be included in respectable society, it is shameful. I am sorry, Little Martha. So sorry."

"Simmons! It is you! Why do you hide from me? I miss you so very much!"

"I am not the one who moved."

A lady dressed in a Roman toga came and tugged Charlotte to her feet. "Charlotte! We have been looking for you everywhere! Come. You must get up and mingle. The game of Costume Couples finished ages ago. Come, there is someone I want you to meet." The toga lady dragged her away.

Martha looked back over her shoulder to Lazarus... his brown eyes burning holes through her disguise and into her heart. "Please stay. Don't leave. I will come back. I will come back," she mouthed urgently as she was tugged away.

But when she did return, his seat was empty of all but the torn wraps of his grave clothes, and the food on his plate was untouched.

"You make a fine picture, sitting here, Miss Charlotte," said Inspector Saunders, as he pulled out his chair from the table to join their group. He was returning to the goldfields for his shift rotation on the morrow. "You brighten the aspect of the room in every way."

"I am pleased you think so," she responded automatically. Charlotte took the plate that was presented to her by a new unfamiliar member of the Redwood team. No longer would wait-staff be faceless, nameless staff to do her bidding. It felt bizarre that she was back here. Her father's party hired Redwood's private dining room while they were guests at the inn for their journey to the gold fields. She had written to Amelia with her intention to visit. When Amelia wrote back, it was a short note, announcing the birth of their son, Wilbur, and briefly mentioned that Simmons had left. He had gone to the Goldfields.

Saunders glanced at her father and adjusted his double-breasted uniform coat. He scratched his greying temple and cleared his throat as he took the napkin from the table. "I am curious why a lady, like yourself, would so emphatically feel the need to visit the goldfields in person. Surely, I can talk you out of it. What would it take, Miss Charlotte, to change your mind towards a diversion that is more in keeping with your refined demeanour? The fields are a coarse and ungainly place."

"Hmm. The Rush is all but exhausted and the area mined out. This is a spectacle that will shortly be an unrecoverable part of our history. To be so close, and never actually set foot there, is a wasted opportunity. I want to see what has captured the imagination of so many, during the time it has been worked over. Be reassured, I have no personal desire to go fossicking."

Her father impatiently took a drink. "The last time you spoke thus... so wistfully of the goldfields, you took a scenic tour and disappeared for months! I trust you are not going to revisit your disappearing act, Charlotte. You had us all in a frenzy of anxiety. And you still have not told me any of what happened."

"But Father, even then, I wrote to you every fortnight and I reassured you of my safety. I promise you, this time I will submit to a full escort the entire time I am there. I don't know how else I can reassure you of my better intentions."

"If you insist on doing this, I will escort you myself."

"You can if you wish... but it is unnecessary, Father. I know you will find it uncomfortable." Charlotte turned to the girl who placed down her bowl and smiled her thanks.

The maid cleared her throat apologetically. "Mistress Amelia offers her regrets for being indisposed this evening, Ma'am. She hopes to see you when you return from your excursion."

"Thank you, Evie. Of course, a young baby is very demanding. Thank you for your care in serving us this evening." The serving girl nodded to her and curtsied.

Her father frowned. "Really, Charlotte... is that necessary? They get their wages."

Charlotte sighed and picked up her serviette, unfolding it in her lap. She had given up trying to broaden the lens of her father. At one time, Mr Willett had demanded only Edwin Couture would be his tailor because his workmanship was outstanding. Yet her father could never accommodate him in his social circle. He never saw any discrepancy in his stance. Trade was in service to his comfort only. They were not people making a difference with skills and abilities. And then her father had been very annoyed when Couture sold his tailoring business to a man who was less particular in his work, because of the inconvenience that was to his wardrobe. Charlotte had heard on the society grapevine, that Edwin Couture recently married a woman of society and means, even if she was plain. Handsome Edwin had quickly traded one mask for another. Charlotte wondered how it was that she had this unyielding curiosity to see the person behind the mask of their profession.

Charlotte proceeded to eat her soup silently. It was thin and flavourless. Well, at least it did confirm one thing. Simmons was definitely not in charge of this kitchen anymore. He would have exposed this offering as dishwater, masquerading as soup, and tossed it down the drain.

She thought again, of her dance at the ball with the masked gentleman with the dark hair. She pictured Simmons play-acting as Lazarus, swathed in his grave clothes, sipping his drink through a slit in the wrappings; his glove hiding the scar on his hand once more. She imagined him, leaning over his roasting pan, his dark hair tied back with his bandana; the intensity of his gaze focused as he applied the basting brush over the duck with precision. She saw him take a breath before he cut her hair with a bold unconventional sweep of the shears. He had offered his admiration and said it suited her. Edwin only saw the offense to convention, and the interruption to his plan. She felt Simmons sitting beside her on the cold flagstone floor, in the kitchen as she bared her broken heart, and he had soothed her with the kindness of a friend who refused to pretend.

Refused to pretend. Yes... Simmons took off his mask when he was in his kitchen. It was at those times she had seen him without pretence. How was it that she finally recognised him, when he donned a mask at a ball, or was encased in a costume at a party? That confused her endlessly. She thought about it constantly. Had she also allowed her mask to slip? Had he truly seen her as he asserted? He supposed the humble Martha to be more noteworthy than Charlotte in her elegant ball gown. Now that he had seen both, was that true? She needed to answer that question. That was why she was here.

⁕⁕⁕

The next morning, a buggy took them out to the goldfields, taking the road up through the Gilyard Mountain pass. It was a slow trip. The rough road through the range was well travelled. There were many pedestrians on the narrow road, pushing their barrows and carrying their swags. As their buggy passed by, the diggers moved over to the side of the track and paused to stare. The reports of a new strike, further down the valley meant the dwindling returns from these fields had diggers leaving in droves. Charlotte looked at each face curiously as they passed by, wondering about their story, their families... their ambition. What did it take for them to leave everything, to pursue a life of hardship and discomfort so willingly? There were women as well. More than one barrow carried a toddler in amongst the tin-pans and shovels.

Suddenly, without any preamble, they were in the main camp. Charlotte stepped down from the buggy and took a look around. The landscape was denuded of trees. All along the creek, men had set out their claim to access water which was as valuable as the gold they were searching for. Mining cradles rocked. Sluicing gravel sloshed and grated. Picks clanked harshly, breaking up rock. A dog scrapped and chased a cat in a squall of furry terror across the track. A drunken brawl broke out further down, and quickly attracted a rowdy mob of supporters, egging on each side. It was an overwhelming cacophony of sound. The smell of dirt and sweat and sewage hung around. Canvas tents and slab bark huts had been propped up all along the criss-cross of tracks. There was no sense of order, no sense of permanency.

Her father was impatient to leave. Surely a general survey of the squalor more than sufficiently met the brief his daughter had given. "Father, allow me an excursion down the road a little way, and then we will go," she said. He pursed his lips, covered his nose with a scented kerchief, and frowned at the stubbornness of his daughter. Her mother was never like this. Well, maybe a little. He took a flask from his coat pocket and sought out some shade by the side of a tent where the horses patiently waited, lazily flicking flies from their flanks with their tails.

Charlotte walked along the track with the Peace Officer. Her skirt dragged in the dust; flies buzzed around her hat. She waved them away with the fan on her wrist. It was evident some miners had optimistically dug in for the long haul and were not leaving with the surge of less devoted prospectors moving out. She paused and watched some diggers take a break with a game of cricket. She was amused that their cricket bat was a broad blade shovel; the track was the cricket pitch, and a propped-up barrow served as stumps. The bowler raced in and took a wicket. Those watching raised their bottles and roused a cheer. The bowler accepted the accolades less than humbly with a declaration of victory coloured with a smattering of vivid colloquialisms. His mate nodded towards the inspector and Charlotte who had joined the spectators of their game. The bowler turned around and tipped his hat with a cheeky grin. "Enjoying the show, Ma'am? Petticoat Flat is over yonder... that way..." He pointed out across the creek to a small flat where mounds of mullock merged into the low scrub. Those watching sniggered. His smirk became broader as the shock on her face changed to a flush of red running up her neck. None too subtly, he was letting her know that since men were not allowed over there on the designated woman's flat, it also followed that women should not loiter here. She felt his leer cover her fashionable attire; it didn't look like she would be hitching up her skirts to join those women prospecting for gold along Petticoat Flat.

Inspector Saunders stepped forward. "Mind your manners, Jackson," he warned, "or I'll be checking your licence permits... again. It has to be on your person at all times."

"I've got my paper..." he said with a surly curl of his lip.

"Perhaps you won't find it."

The game went silent, and the players stared in churlish defiance, standing elbow to elbow, until Charlotte gathered the inspector's arm, and encouraged him to move on.

"Inspector? It may seem like a very odd request for me to come here, but I do have my reasons."

"No doubt you do, Miss. The diggings are a curiosity for sure, but this is no place for a lady."

She soberly nodded. "Yes, I see that. But I came to investigate a matter... to give it my personal attention. I wanted to try and locate an associate... the brother of a family friend." Well, that was sort of true. Lazarus was the brother of Martha. "The officers do not have time to address the worry. I understand that the heartbreak of my friend cannot be a priority when they are so pressed with official business. I trust you appreciate my reluctance to disclose this matter to my father. It would seem unreasonable to him. Feminine curiosity for a spectacle seems more acceptable," she said soberly.

"Without being presumptuous, Miss, the excursion seems unreasonable to me as well." But he nodded. The absurdity in her wanting to come here now made more sense: tracking a family friend. This was not an uncommon quest, families desperately trying to locate missing sons, and brothers, and nephews... those who sought fortune and disappeared in the pursuit of it. Mr Willett requested the same thing of him when Charlotte went missing.

The inspector nodded to the officer on security detail outside the slab hut that acted as the site office. This little room held the licencing records. The desk was a makeshift platform balanced on boxes that were jammed full of files. It was primitive and rough, but even Charlotte admitted it was a better set-up than what most were camping in. Saunders pulled out a folder and leafed through it until he located a slip: S. L. Simmons. He noted the license number and cross referenced it to a site ledger of the claims. They walked over the road, and along a low track running along the creek. There were channels dug to divert water from the creek to various claims. Charlotte asked around. Seth Simmons? But no one had heard of the name. Not that they were very attentive to their questions. There had been a collapse in the shaft over on the rise. Mates had lost their lives.

"I'm sorry, Ma'am. It is very likely that he's moved on. There is really no way to track 'em. If people want to be left alone... this is the place to do it," Saunders said as he returned his ledger to the office and shoved it back in its box. "You can tell your friend that we tried..."

He hesitated and picked up a report on the desk; some rough notes scribbled on a page; it was the summary of the shaft collapse. Three bodies recovered; two known men were not brought to the surface. He read out the third name. S. L. Simmons. The number beside his name matched the license. Critically injured. Expired of injuries before medical help could intervene. No known kin. He showed her the paper. It was dated the day before yesterday.

Charlotte gasped. "Two days?" Her eyes lost focus. Her knees gave way and she fell to the floor, gasping. "Surely not! I cannot be too late..." The inspector quickly supported her slight frame as he offered her a stump in the corner to sit on. He poured her a mug of water from a jug sitting beside her... turbid and warm... and he encouraged her to drink. Inspector Saunders stood there awkwardly for a time fanning her face in the heat. Finally, he cleared his throat. "Ma'am, I am so sorry. This is indeed difficult news to give to your friend. Are you okay, Miss?"

She took a shuddering breath. No! She was not okay. Nothing would ever be okay again. She stood to her feet and closed her eyes against the glare as they emerged from the hut. Her father was still swatting flies by the buggy. "Thank you, Inspector. I'm ready to go back now."

⁘

13.

Charlotte stepped into her bath and tried to soak off the layers
and layers of dust, and the smell that had infiltrated the very pores of
her skin. She was not sure how long she stayed there. Someone knocked
on the door. "Yes?"

"Miss? Mrs Bailey sent me to check on you... to make sure you
were, okay?"

Charlotte quickly flushed her face with water that was now
cold. This was a grief that could not be shared. "Evie, I lost track of
time. Please give my apologies to my father that I will not be joining
Mister and Missus Bailey for dinner tonight. I am not feeling well." She
stepped out of the bath and wrapped a towel around her. How could
she have thought that such a quest would bring any clarity to the
confusion that haunted her? Oh, but this time it did. It was clear. Her
story was a repetitive tale; a doomed account of unrequited love where
chapter after chapter, the pointless pattern of her efforts was emerging.
She had not seen the man worthy of her affection because of her blind
devotion to another. In the end, Edwin proved so undeserving... and
Simmons... well... Simmons was Simmons. More tears.

After the time when dinner would have been finished, there
was another knock. "Your father, Mr Willett, is here to see you, Miss."
Evie ushered him into the room, and she placed a small soup tray on
Charlotte's dressing table.

Her father stood for a time, wordless. Eventually he cleared his
throat. "Charlotte, Charlotte, I don't understand. This morning you

were in a fever of anticipation for the diversion of the goldfields. Now you are unwell?"

"Yes, Father. I don't want to travel back just yet."

"I should have been firmer against your insistence to travel to the diggings. It is obvious such squalor would put your health in danger. You have always had such a delicate constitution."

"Rest, I think... rest will be best for me. But I do understand you have matters to attend to. I am going to speak to Mrs Bailey and spend a few days here to recover." She sneezed to give weight to her plight.

"Here? But for how long? Should I send for Phillips?"

"No doctor will be necessary. I'll probably be my usual self in a week. I really could not face the trip at the moment." She openly acknowledged to herself, that was a bold-faced lie. What she could not face was the ritual of being okay... or enduring everyone's scrutiny if she declared she was not.

"But will you get the attention you deserve in a place like this, my Dear?"

"Mrs Bailey has assigned Evie to my room. You can see she has been very attentive, Father. She drew a very nice bath for me this evening... and see... she has even delivered soup... unbidden." That part was true. Being left alone was her additional hope.

"Well, okay. I will send one of the men to collect you directly. Say Friday?"

"No need, Father. It would be far better for me to make my own way home. Then I will not inconvenience anyone if there is a delay. I will give you updates and let you know how I am recuperating. The Bailey's have transport going into town on a regular basis to pick up supplies. I'm sure they can accommodate another passenger."

"A goods cart! Really Charlotte, how do you even know this? Your Mother would die of worry if she had not already passed on."

"Father, I mean no disrespect to Mother's devotion, nor her memory. I assure you I will be fine." She just wanted silence. Silence to wrap around her grief in comfort... but it seemed there was no comfort to be had.

⁂

Charlotte dressed and walked down the stairs of Redwood Inn. There was resolve in her hand that slid along the banister. For four days she had locked herself away and allowed herself the privilege of deep mourning. She knew, once she emerged, she would have to set aside such liberties. If no one knew of her secret devotion, how could they understand the extent of her heartache? She would never be sure that even Simmons knew of it before he was crushed in that shaft collapse. Did he understand their cryptic murmurings at a costume party? She took a shuddering breath. Simmons had encouraged and blown into life the flame of the grown-up in her, just like he fanned the oven fires that cooked his amazing dishes. Inadvertently he had equally fanned to life the flame of her regard.

As she stepped down the staircase, she took another deep breath. This is what she needed to do. She needed to stand up and find her own dream, rather than constantly chase the rainbow of being someone else's dream. She needed to discover if there was anything that made her eyes come alive with the passion she saw in Simmons as he painted his roasted duck with plum glaze. But right now, as her eyes clouded again with tears, she could not imagine they would ever again light with laughter, much less passion.

Charlotte had only ever been taught that her destiny was to love a person wearing a distinguished suit and a fashionable hat. She sighed. She, at least, could make the distinction now. The right social connections did not make the right moral fibre. Cyrus was devoted... until the next pretty face came along. She knew being married to him would not change that. Edwin had the jacket and the felt hat, but not the character to go with it. An evening coat with tails did not mean sincere devotion. His clothes were a mask, acting a part to seduce her money into marrying him. She had defied all family expectations when she allowed Edwin into her heart. She believed that crossing that wide social divide was evidence of the strength of her great love. But it wasn't evidence of anything. A great love would never die so quickly, nor be replaced so promptly, or be forgotten so rapidly. Did she even have the capacity to love the way that Simmons had? What would light her eyes, with the same energy she saw when Simmons focused placing the last layer of pumpkin ginger cake on his Homestead Baklava?

Evie dipped a curtsy. "Ma'am, Mrs Bailey has requested you join them for their family dinner." Charlotte tilted her head and looked into Evie's nervous face. She realised something then. People were her passion. The tentative smile that Evie offered as she was putting down a soup bowl did more to feed her soul than the menu that was served. Connecting with people of any station... all stations... seeing underneath their mask. Whatever colour or form it came in. Regardless of their status or occupation. Perhaps she had not seen Simmons because her own mask shrouded her vision.

Well, she would try to correct her line of sight. Death sometimes brings the greatest clarity. Pain had certainly amplified her feeling. She was surprised by that. She thought it would numb or dull or mute her senses... but as she pulled out the chair at the dining table, she was suddenly aware that she was, in fact, still alive. Simmons had given her something to bring life out of the tomb once more. He still offered her hope. Her task was to nurture that hope into strength. To unbind it and let it move freely. She would take her cue from Simmons and draw a lesson from the Master who transformed a wedding with a miracle, moving a catering disaster beyond mediocre, to extraordinary. The same Master who performed a miracle at a funeral, drawing life back from death and allowing that life to flourish. She would work towards excellence like that, regardless of who noticed it, or those who didn't.

Amelia sat as Bailey pulled out her chair. "Little Wilbur is settled with Lolly. I'm glad you can join us, as today is a special day," Amelia announced to the small number of guests around the table. "Today is the anniversary of when I met Maurice. He was sitting all mysteriously behind his desk... surrounded by all his books. I thought I had walked right into a magical world." She giggled and turned to him. "Perhaps I did."

"And I thought an angel had glided into my very grim office. It was like you turned the light on, my lovely wife."

"Soon you will have more time for your books again. You never really have time to enjoy the library here at Redwood. The travellers, that come to and fro from the Goldfields take up so much of your time. Perhaps the reports of the goldfields giving out are actually true, since the number of travellers is becoming less and less."

"I suspect the reports will be proven right. I hope that doesn't mean we will be off the map completely though. Travellers bring business. Eloise, do not play in your food or you can go back to the nursery with Lolly and the babies."

Her blonde curls bobbed, and her little lip quivered. "Hami plays in his food..."

Amelia patted her little hand and fondly spoke. "Yes, I know Dearest, but Hamilton is still little... even though he is not as little as baby Wilbur. But when they are big like you, they both will have to learn manners as well."

Charlotte focused on her soup and tried to smother the waves of grief that unaccountably surfaced. How could she explain such a thing? She finished quickly, and stood up and cleared the table, putting the dishes on the sideboard. She paused in horror, as she realised her presumption, and then let out her breath as she registered that no one here minded. What a relief that was. No one rebuked her; no one told her to sit down. No one prompted her to mind her manners. No one reminded her of her responsibility to be elegant. If the standard of appropriate etiquette was simply not playing with her food, then that was an enormous reprieve.

"Eloise, perhaps I can help you?" Charlotte said with conspirator's whisper, as she sat back down. "Can I tell you a secret?" she asked.

Eloise nodded, and her fair hair cascaded around her little round face, her eyes downcast.

"I like to play with my food too. But when I am with company, I know that is not allowed... so I try something else. I play a game called, *Catch the Flavours*. Do you know what a flavour is? It is all the wonderful things that makes food taste special. Sometimes the flavour is well hidden it is hard to find. Sometimes it just explodes in your mouth, and we have to be very careful to hold it in. So... can we play together when the next part of our meal is served?"

"You are the pretty lady that Cook likes, aren't you?"

Charlotte smiled sadly, tears springing to her lashes. "Oh, that is so sweet. I liked him too."

"Why are you sad?"

"Because I miss him very much... and I don't think I ever told him that. So, I think it is a very good idea that we distract ourselves with a game of *Catch the Flavours*. Here come the plates... are we ready?" She got up and helped take the bowls to the table, from the little trolley that Mrs Pearson pushed in. There was roast lamb and an assortment of vegetables. It was an ordinary rendition compared to what Simmons would deliver, but it was adequate. While Bailey carved the roast, she helped serve out the vegetables as Eloise directed her with the number of pieces. "So, the game goes like this: you have to choose just one food... meat or vegetable?"

"Veggegable..." Her blond hair nodded.

"Okay, now so very carefully, take one piece. We close our lips, and we notice the flavour in our mouth. Can you catch it?"

She nodded very enthusiastically speaking around a mouth full of carrot. "Oh yes! It tastes Carrottie. Very Carrottie!"

"Oh!" said Charlotte with sparkling eyes. "I think I caught it too! What would you like to catch next?" Eloise pointed to the roast lamb. "Sometimes there are so many different flavours to catch... the meat, or the herbs, or perhaps gravy."

Her eyes grew wide with admiration. "I have a secret too," confessed Eloise. "I want Cook to come back. His food has more favvours to catch..."

"Oh..." sighed Charlotte with a gasp. "He really did." She pushed her plate aside and stood up, gathering her plate and the serving dishes and putting them on the sideboard. Her head started the thump. She imagined the soil pinning him down... and felt the inertia of her grief making it impossible to move. She was suffocating, trapped in a tunnel as well. How could she ever escape this?

It was evident that staying here was no longer a good idea. She had just thought... She closed her eyes, stinging with tears. After her mother's funeral, there had been such an outpouring of condolences and gentle consideration. If she wanted to sit in the drawing room in her mother's favourite chair... she sat there. If she wanted to walk in the garden looking over her mother's primroses and violets... she walked there. But here, she didn't have access to these familiar rituals. No one could acknowledge her loss because no one knew of it. She had told her father she had a cold to explain her swollen eyes and red nose. She had hoped she would feel closer to Simmons here as she said her farewells. But it seemed all that had happened was that her pain was multiplied by a secret that was never going to change.

So, in the light of this awareness, she decided then, that it was better to bite the bullet and submit to the inevitable. The unavoidable reality was she needed to resume her life as a grown-up. That thought made her shudder. Simmons had talked so openly about these things. She knew no one else who dared to traverse personal territories so frankly. How could two people cover so much terrain in a few months over pots and pans, washing-up water, basting brushes and rolling pins? She sat back down at the table, closed her eyes and rubbed the tension along her hairline with her fingertips. This was ridiculous! Even her hair, short and unstylish, was a reminder. It was not pinned smooth because it had been cut in her desperate attempt to stay hidden. Then she had wanted to hide... but now... now she desperately wanted someone to see her.

She opened her eyes as Mrs Pearson put down the dessert pedestal covered with a matching ceramic cake cover.

"A special dessert, Ma'am."

"Lovely! What a wonderful way to celebrate our anniversary!" Amelia smiled gloriously and looked like Christmas had come early. Eloise sat up tall and clapped excitedly. Mrs Pearson lifted the cover and there, drenched in a delicious glaze of sticky treacle sauce, was a Homestead Baklava. Charlotte's eyes flew open in shock. She put her elbows on the table... closed her eyes... and covered her forehead. This was getting so out of control!

14.

Charlotte shook her head and opened her eyes carefully. It still stood there, layered, and sweet and tantalizing on the cake stand. There was a wedge cut out, revealing the layers interspersed with sweet date filling. No one could make this except... Was it possible?

She squeezed her eyes shut again. Or was this someone's version of a memorial? No. He said it was his own recipe that he never shared... a tribute to his mother. This had to be! When she opened her eyes, she stared at Amelia who was giggling with Bailey, and Eloise was squirming, unable to contain herself.

"Cook says it is a special dessert for the lady," said Mrs Pearson looking directly at Charlotte.

"Can we tempt you?" ask Amelia happily. "You haven't eaten anything for days. We thought this..."

She jumped up and bolted out the door. Charlotte ran down the corridor and rushed into the kitchen. Simmons was not there. The replacement Cook frowned, shaking her head as she took off her apron and dumped it in the basket by the door. She muttered to the scullery maid as they both disappeared out the back. Charlotte stared around the empty kitchen breathing hard, wishing this torture would end. Just when she had resolved her feelings, there he was... resurrected once more. This too had been an illusion. He was not here after all.

She turned to go when a voice spoke. "Little Martha? You have come."

She spun around. His bandana was tied over his brow, he was coming from the pantry, with a wine bottle and two glasses in his hand.

He turned to indicate two serves of cake on the bench, waiting. He didn't smile, he didn't tease. But he proceeded to pour the glasses, his eyes locked on her. "A wine with your dessert, Little Martha?"

She shook her head vigorously. "How can you be here? Is this a game?"

"Why would you think I am playing with you?"

"Amelia said you had gone to the Goldfields. So, I went up there. Inspector Saunders showed me the report of the shaft collapse... five men. Two unrecovered. Your name was on the list."

His brown eyes narrowed slightly, creasing around the edges as he frowned. "You went to the fields... looking for me?"

She glared at him severely. "Amelia said... I saw the report. Your name was on the list!" she accused again.

"You did. You went up there. You were following your heart... Little Martha." His face, tight with tension, relaxed slightly. Less grim.

"Was it a test, so that I would think you were killed? Why would you go to such lengths?"

"Oh Martha. No. I finally had word that my cousin was probably there after all. I went out there to check it out. I found him. I did... but Lenny wanted to stay lost. He didn't want to come home."

"That was your cousin? The name on the list was S. Simmons. How can Lenny be S. Simmons?"

"Well, it is. Stanley Leonard. That's him. I was about to return when the collapse happened. I got to him in time. I wasn't too late... but he still would not leave. He went back in for his mates... a second collapse took him. In the space of a few days... he could have been coming home with me. I have to go and give word to my aunt. I don't know how to tell her that..." He shook his head bewildered. "I stayed to bury him... and his mates. When I came in last night, Amelia mentioned you were here, but that you had locked yourself away and weren't eating. No one said you thought I was in the slide."

"I didn't tell anyone that I went there to find you."

He sat down on his stool and helped himself to one of the pieces of cake. He handed her a cake fork without any comment and continued to eat.

She stood there holding the fork, staring at him, hardly able to know what to think. "Can you not understand what that was like for me... thinking you were lost forever?"

"Oh, I know. I am familiar with that feeling. I knew that feeling when you declared that you were to be married to that social highbrow named Dempsey. Then, when it seemed that I was given a reprieve, I felt it again when you declared you were in love with some fancy-dressing imbecile named Edwin. I felt it again when you went away without saying goodbye. Little Martha, you do not have dibs on feeling abandoned in the depth of your feeling."

"Is that why you did it... is that why you came to the ball and the costume party... to extract revenge on my poorly tempered heart? To torment me?"

"On both occasions you were surrounded by people in disguise. If you were fortunate enough to encounter one who offered you attention, why do you suppose it was me? It could have been anyone. He might be still out there."

"I know. I know it was you!"

"How could you know such a thing?"

"You do not play fair, Seth Simmons! You stand before me... something I have dreamed of for months, only to find you hidden behind a mask. You were less masked at the ball, when our faces were covered. No, you do not play fair at all! Why would you hide from me now?"

"Is this me hiding? Or is this being more transparently honest than we have ever been? Little Martha, you let me go... on both occasions. You willingly suffer the indignity of being a scullery maid for months for a tailor, but you would not even try to detain me for an evening together. I doubt you have the feeling you declare." He shrugged and went back to eating his cake.

"You know I feel. I feel so much that it pains me! I tried on both occasions to find you. It is not that I let you go; it is that you left!"

"I would have stayed if you had asked me to."

"But I did! How can you say that? I explicitly said..."

"Little Martha. You are not my Edwin, where I will dally around at your convenience waiting for months, until you can find the time. A relationship of equality has nothing to do with social standing or occupation. No one gets to call all the shots. There is a difference between being asked to stay; and being told wait in the corner like a dog. I am not your pet project."

She came and stood before him, tears pooling on her lashes. "Seth, I am so sorry if I showed you disrespect. But I don't want to lose you now... not after all this time. I am in shock, and I am in a fever of worry. It is like you are resurrected for me. Lazarus, you have come back to me from the dead."

He paused... and put down his cake fork. He reached out and pulled her to his side, as he sat before her on the stool. Her little frame met him eye to eye, tears rolled down her cheeks. "Little Martha, I am also in shock and in a fever of worry. Pulling Lenny out of the rubble like that... it has shaken me... and perhaps that comes out in ugly ways. I am sorry to distress you so. There will be no miracle of resurrection for him."

"Oh Seth... I am so sorry. What a terrible thing."

He pulled his bandana from his forehead and gently wiped her cheek. "Oh Martha. Please don't take it to mean I am not pleased you are here. I am."

"I've made mistakes. I know it! How could I not see you when you were in front of me for so long? But I once said you have a deep capacity to hold a great love. When you came to the ball... traversing the social divide in a way I thought was impossible, I thought it meant... I thought that you would choose me as your great love. Please tell me... am I mistaken? Have I imagined all this?"

He smiled sadly. Grief still in his eyes. "No, Little Martha, you have not imagined this. If you feel I am resurrected... to me, it feels is like *we* have been given a second chance at life. I told you before, I never made a declaration of love, and I didn't make it before because it seemed hopeless. But I will make it now. What I feel for you, how we are together, makes the love I have for cooking seem juvenile. I love you, Little Martha. I truly do."

Martha stood there and suddenly her silent tears burst in a flood. A weight lifted from her chest so abruptly that she sobbed at the relief. Simmons gathered her in his arms and held her tight. "Shh. I am sorry I have grieved you. So sorry. Little Martha, forgive me..."

Her little frame melted into his chest, and she could hear his heartbeat racing. She clung there for a long while, not daring to move, not willing to let him go. Eventually he prized her back... a sober look over his face. "I promise not to disappear again. I am here. You can unwrap me now, so you can see me." He tilted her chin and smiled. "And if I am not mistaken, Little Martha, your mask has slipped. I see you too..." and he kissed her in an explosion of passion.

15

Nolan ushered them into the dim drawing room, and Aunt Prudence indicated with a regal wave of her hand, that they were to sit on a hard, tapestried lounge. "Who have you brought with you Seth? Why would you bring a stranger to my house?"

"Aunt Prudence, this is Charlotte Willett."

"Willett, you say? Are you related to the Willetts from Grosvenor Estate?"

"Yes Ma'am. Albert Willett is my father."

"Humph." Aunt Prudence eyes narrowed as she looked over her nose at Charlotte. "You are about as dull as all the reports I have heard. What are you doing here with him?" Charlotte felt herself shrink under her severe appraisal. She stammered and squirmed, and felt like Eloise being reprimanded for playing with her food. She tried to formulate a response, but no words would come.

Simmons cleared his throat. "Aunt, I am escorting her home. It is unfortunate, but I do not come socially to introduce you to my friend. I carry some sad news."

Aunt Prudence turned and directed her stare at his face, and then grunted. "I doubt that hesitating to deliver your message will change bad news to good. Just get it over with. I suspect I already know what you have to tell me."

"You do? Oh. I am so sorry, Aunt."

"I imagine you found him, and he refused to return with you. He has not changed his mind and insists on staying estranged. Am I correct?"

"Partly. I did find Lenny and I did speak with him... and as you suppose... he wanted to stay working his claim with the syndicate he had formed with his mates."

"Well, it can't be helped. You made contact. That is more than the professional investigators whom I hired were able to accomplish. Your obligation to me is completed. But no doubt you could have tried a little harder to dissuade him from staying."

Simmons adjusted his collar. "There is more. There was a collapse in the shaft where he and his partners were working. He went back in, to try and extract those who were trapped. I could not stop him."

Aunt Prudence stared at him for a long time. The line of her mouth went firmer... harder. "What are you saying Seth? Could not... or would not?"

"One and the same. He was determined. Aunt Prudence, there was another slide in the shaft. Lenny didn't make it. He died a hero trying to save those he worked with."

"A hero? You call grubbing around in the dirt like some hairless mole the nature of a hero?"

"I call the character of a man who would not abandon his mates in an unexpected tragedy, truly honourable."

"Mates! He shows fidelity to casual associates who have no blood rights, and yet he forsakes his own mother? That is not the substance of valour!"

"Aunt, I am truly sorry I do not bring more reasonable news for you."

She paused and poured herself a cup of tea from a pot sitting on a tray by her side. Her hand shook as she took a sip, and her fine china cup rattled in its saucer. "Psft! You think you are being generous telling me this version of events. But I know Leonard. He had an incurable dalliance with a devil called Gold. It was a ridiculous obsession that never made sense: he inherited more than he would ever find prospecting. No, he was lost to me a long time ago."

"I am sorry, Aunt."

"It is indeed a cruel blow of fate. Leonard is my only son... and he throws his potential away and dies an anonymous digger in a pitfall. I am not stupid. If officials have not brought this news to my door as his kin, it means he refused to acknowledge me. And yet, here *you* are, the illegitimate bastard of an unwed whore... and you show all the level-headed sense of a gentleman heir." She put down her cup. "I think we are done here. Good day."

"You reached out to me, Aunt Prudence. This was your idea. I remind you that we negotiated an exchange. You committed to providing three acts of influence for me if I would investigate this matter for you. You said that you would offer influence in my menial world so lacking in consequence. The first would be credited when I pledged my commitment to the task. The second on following leads to where Lenny might be. The third on actually making contact with him."

"Congratulations. You have done your part. Our contract is complete. Now leave."

"You've completed two acts on my behalf. There is another act of influence still on the ledger that is unfulfilled."

"You despicable filth of a wanton wench! How dare you use my tragedy to extract more."

"It is what we agreed."

"I have completed my part. You got your ticket to the Willett's Charity Ball." She glared significantly at Charlotte sitting at his side.

"Yes, you obtained it – that was the first act of influence."

"I also secured the catering job for the fundraiser party as you asked and negotiated your bizarre participation with whatever ridiculous costumed role you insisted on, as part payment for the job. Mrs Jensen said she would only contract further business with you according to her satisfaction of the experience. It is not my fault you cannot hold your own in a world that expects more class than billy-tea, damper, and treacle."

"That was understood – influence two."

"And still, you want more? You cold-hearted pitiless reptile. You have no compassion for the distress imposed on me by this tragedy."

"I think it is family trait, Aunt Prudence. Regardless of the outcome, you committed to three influences."

"You come to tell me my son is dead! I would prefer to hear he is alive and living in squalor! This voids the terms of our agreement."

"I don't intend to present it today. After all, you have been given distressing news. However, I do intend to have you deliver on what we agreed. I will return on the fortnight to let you know what I require."

"It is a shame you are a hopeless sewer rat, with no virtue or linage to speak of. You would have done well with the right upbringing and schooling."

"As you conveniently remind me, Aunt, with such convincing airs when you want my assistance, we are still blood. We will take our leave now, but I will return on the fortnight to discuss the third influence." Simmons stood up. He offered Charlotte his arm and they left.

⁂

16.

They sat in the tea gardens and Simmons ordered a Devonshire tea for both of them. Apart from that, he said nothing for a long while. Eventually, Charlotte put down her cup. "Are you alright?"

Simmons blinked. "I hardly know. I find audiences with my aunt provoking to the extreme. I struggle to hold my own whenever I am there, and it always takes some time for me to recover. Just sitting in her drawing room makes me feel like I am in a narrow pipe, gushing a fast torrent of water. And although I don't allow myself to get swept away, it feels dangerous and exhausting. Every time, without fail, I am holding on for dear life."

"Then why insist that she keeps to her agreement. Now you are committed to going back."

"She gets away with such a lot by having a pout and throwing out vile, obnoxious insults. I am one person who holds her to account. I remind myself that I do have an advantage in my relationship with my aunt that no one else has. She doesn't like me. And although I am the only family she has left, I know she will never change her mind on that. The upside of this is: I don't have to try and win points with her. Besides, she is not wrong. Her influences have been useful." He smiled. "I had a dance with the Belle of the Ball, Little Martha."

She returned his smile and blushed slightly. "That was what I would call a 'swept off my feet' moment."

"Then it was worth every aggravating conversation I endured to secure the privilege of that ticket."

"The message you left in the mask has haunted me... in a beautiful way...

Simmons nodded. "Ahh, Paul Dunbar. That is from one of his recent poems. He hits the nail on the head with sublime simplicity."

"I was surprised you know Dunbar's work. He is making quite a splash in London society. They say Dunbar's parents were escaped slaves, from the American civil war. He has remarkable mastery of prose and poem."

Simmons shrugged. "Dunbar offers me unique inspiration. He's managed to cross the social divide... black to white; slave to free; poor to comfortable. He did that, not by buying his way or hiding the truth... but by being ruthlessly honest, and offering to share his unique art. I think I appreciate his poetry because his insight is like a reduction on my stove... all the flavour concentrated in a small literary sauce."

She smiled. "I played a game with Eloise the other night... *Catch the Flavours.* I have not always given myself time to catch the flavours of what I consume. But I've played with the flavours of this poem. They are potent... unpleasant almost. It is true that I also wear a mask. With a bleeding heart I also smile."

"Therein lies the risk, Little Martha. Do we dare show ourselves?" He put down his cup. He took another bite of his scone piled with strawberry jam. His eyes were serious. "Little Martha... there are some things you should know if you are willing to hear them. I would let you see me without my mask. But I warn you, what you may find is potent and unpleasant. Aunt Prudence has already alluded to the severity of it." Charlotte raised her brow and said nothing as he continued. "What I need to tell you is quite shocking. I suspect, it is more shocking than anything that bloodhound Edwin ever put forward. But with a full disclosure you can decide if you will consider keeping company with me." She went to object, but he held up his hand. "Just hold your judgement until you know the extent of it."

She nodded, and awkwardly swallowed a mouthful of tea.

He took a deep breath. "I hardly know where to start. My mother's name was Rosemary Mitchell. She was from a well-educated background and a respectable family, but when she was nineteen, she was discovered pregnant. She refused to expose the father and her family would have nothing further to do with her. Mother found a considerate family who gave her a position as a cook. She married a drover, Holt Greenwood, for his name before I was born, and essentially never saw him again. So, you were right, I was raised in a kitchen while my mother worked. Long hours and long years. She taught me how to cook, to play the violin, to love poetry and how to dance. She was my governess and my schoolteacher. Quite gifted, actually, in anything she set her mind to. In our entire twisted family, my mother was an exceptional jewel. She devoted her life to me and was determined that a kitchen would not impede my education or my opportunities. I grew up here in the valley... over at Yellow Creek Station. My mother tutored the Hansen daughters over peeling potatoes and braising mutton steaks. They were much older than me... but because I was tall... I became dance homework. She made me sit in on all of their lessons. After Mr Hansen passed, a cousin came from the city to take over the station. Mother was devoted to the family after all they had done for her, so she left the valley with Mrs Hansen."

There was a long pause while they distractedly watched some butcher birds dance around the tables waiting to be given castoffs from morning tea plates. "Everyone in Mother's previous life cut ties with her, except her sister, Prudence. They were close growing up, and she kept in contact with her. After Mother left, Prudence married a man named Arthur. The kicker is... Arthur Simmons is not only my uncle... he is also my father. Mother told me they were in love. But when she became pregnant, they could not marry because of the scandal, so she disappeared. It was then that Mr Arthur Simmons... the upstanding swine that he was, married my mother's sister, Prudence. This means... Lenny is not my cousin... he is actually my brother. I didn't just pull my cousin from the rubble. I was trying to save my little brother. And I was unable to do it." His frown drew taut across his brow, and he stared into his cup.

"Oh, Seth..." She hardly knew where to focus. She reached out and touched his hand. His hand twitched under her fingers as she felt the rough burn scar along the back of his hand. The marks looked darker under the shadows of the trees where they sat, and she wondered how deep some scars lie.

A butcher bird was eyeing off his plate, so he threw some crumbs onto the ground, and Simmons watched him swoop in for the titbit. "In a moment of weakness, Mother disclosed all this to her sister... and Prudence, quite simply, has never forgiven her... or me. Mother's lingering sadness when she died was that they were never reconciled. But I remind myself, my mother was still Prudence's sister, regardless of her circumstances. I think Prudence already knew that she was never really loved by her husband, and then she had an explanation for it. So, she continues to rub my sewer-rat status in my face, until she needs something. Then she plays the family card. Prudence never acknowledges our brotherhood... Lenny and I were always officially estranged cousins... but in the tradition of this family, convenience and appearance are the higher order of things." He took a deep breath and another drink of tea. "That is why I took the position at Redwood. Because it is on the way to the goldfields. I could extract the best information on where Lenny might have gone from there. To start with I had no interest in Aunt Prudence or her agenda... I was only looking for my brother. Redwood was a long shot at best... but it was the most substantial lead I'd had."

Simmons finished his cup and poured himself another. "Another tradition of this family is that all the men are called by their second names. Leonard *Arthur* Simmons. Stanley *Leonard* Simmons. Seth *Simmons* Greenwood. Of course, Aunt Prudence refuses to acknowledge that convention, since it is her husband's family name and their tradition, so she insists on calling me Seth. I think she is the only one who does."

"Greenwood? Your surname is Greenwood? Not Simmons?"

"This is true."

"Oh. I started calling you Seth, because I thought using your Christian name was more respectful... rather than just using your surname like some servant. Oh..." She blinked hard and stared at him. "So, I would be Mrs Greenwood... not Mrs Simmons?"

He looked at her and smiled. "Also, true. Out of all that I have said... this is what you come away with? What name you will carry if we marry?"

"Not if... when. I do intend to marry you Mr Greenwood. You have allowed me to see you without a mask. That trust is more important to me than all the *grins and lies* that other, less shocking, suitors offer. Besides, I could not possibly give up having a Homestead Baklava made for me, now I have discovered the source of it."

"You value the experience so much... that you would marry to keep it, even in the controversy?"

She looked deep into his brown eyes. "Oh yes, I value it very, very much... and I think marriage is the only reasonable course that I have to protect my interest in this matter, shocking controversy or not."

"Is this a proposal? Would you come and traverse the changing landscapes of life with me?"

"Oh, it is not a proposal...that would be entirely improper. But you will know when and where, to make such a declaration."

"Hmm. I was right after all. I will definitely require this third act of influence. If it was not for you, Little Martha, I would not have allowed Aunt Prudence any interference in my life at all. See, in the spirit of my rather maladjusted and twisted family, I can also hold to the principle of convenience."

"Then it sounds to me, Seth Simmons Greenwood, that you have a plan."

"Oh, you are an odd one, Little Martha. You really are." He shook his head in bewilderment. "I really did not think that this would be the outcome of this masks-off, honest little conversation over a Devonshire tea. You are completely unexpected, Little Martha." And he picked up her hand and pressed it to his lips. "So full of surprises."

17.

Aunt Prudence leaned hard on the footman's arm and climbed into the carriage. "Good afternoon, Aunt Prudence. Glad you could make time to meet with me," said Simmons quietly from the shadows of the carriage as she sat heavily on the seat.

She lifted her chin, and the severe line of her mouth remained firm. "So, you bribed the footman to give you entry to my carriage for an audience. It is merely indicative of how desperate your case is."

"No bribe required. All that was needed was to ask him. He was particularly obliging. His kindness was convenient since you refused me entry by conventional means. I've been trying to secure this appointment for over a week now."

"Kindness never gets one anywhere. If you were candid, you would realise influence comes at a price, and kindness is not part of the equation."

"And yet, the case-in-point is that I am here talking to you... secured by being considerate to Nolan, who has been your steward for many years. He outgrew the position of footman years ago, and yet you still insist on calling him that."

"It would not do for the man to get airs. And your 'kindness', nor his, will not be so celebrated when the footman and his family are thrown out onto the street for insubordination. See where kindness gets him then."

"The lengths that you go to, Prudence, never cease to shock me. Your issues are with me, not Nolan. Leave him out of it."

"My issue is with anyone who does not abide by my rules."

"And one of your rules has been to demonstrate your influence and status so it is universally recognised. You balk at keeping your commitment for the third influence because you guess that it will reach beyond your capability. Securing tickets and catering jobs is sand-play in comparison to what I require this time."

"You suggest I cannot do it? I may not be able to walk on water, but there is little else that I cannot influence."

Simmons looked unconvinced. "Perhaps."

"Humph! Let me be the judge of that. What is it that you need?"

"I want you to convince Albert Willett to give his consent for me to marry his daughter."

She laughed, mirthless and cold. "You little upstart. You will stop at nothing to join the ranks of the respectable."

"You said I could choose whatever I need. This is what I need."

"And what makes you think that Albert Willett would ever give consent for his only daughter to marry the likes of you?"

"You, Aunt Prudence. You make me think that he will do it."

"Really? And why would I drag this respectable family into the mud of your squalor?"

"I am well aware that your word would not be sufficient motivation for this third influence. But I will marry Charlotte. I can do it your way... and protect your name and his. Or I will do it outside those parameters... and you will suffer the humiliation of your family and his family, of having a known connection with me... in all of its shadowed scandal."

"Psft! It is too long ago. It hardly matters anymore."

"Agreed. And if you hardly think it matters, then take that gamble. But scandal buried that deep, grows in the dark to become a monster that can barely be contained. This your chance to control it. Our marriage is no worry for me. I am not ashamed of my mother, and I love Charlotte. So, in this sense, what I offer is merely a courtesy to you. You have the opportunity to retrieve whatever respectability that you think you have and offer the same to Mr Willett. If he is convinced that I am a fitting suitor for his daughter and willingly offers his consent, you Aunt Prudence, will be in the clear. You will be invited to the wedding, but aside from that, you need never hear from me again. But if you do not fulfil your commitment as we agreed, I will make our connection public. Your shame will no longer be hidden. It will be shouted from the rooftops. The gossip columns will lap that up with delicious delight. It will make my cooking reviews seem bland in comparison. That, Aunt Prudence, is my hand. That is what I will play."

Her eyes narrowed. She went quiet. "For someone who says he upholds the value of 'kindness', this is not what I consider sympathetic in any way."

"My sympathy is for Nolan. I expect you to retain him, with no consequence to his employment. The man has been faithful to you for twenty-five years. Why he insists on staying with you is beyond me. Don't cut off your nose to spite me, Aunt. Nolan stays."

There was another long pause. "Very well. This is how it will play out. It will take some time to organise, so do not be in a hurry. But you can be sure that you will have your consent by the end of the month."

⁂

18.

Aunt Prudence adjusted her weight in the chair as she heard Nolan answer the front door. She waited for him to come into the drawing room to announce the visitors. She didn't stand, but regally made their welcome be known, as she nodded and rested her book in her lap.

"Mr Willett. What a pleasure. So nice that you and your daughter would join me this evening. On the off-season of the social calendar, I become weary in trying to sort through appropriate social engagements. Your invitation to afternoon tea was a genteel and generous gesture. It is a relief to have made your acquaintance. Thank you for allowing me to return your hospitality this evening."

"It is our pleasure, Mrs Simmons," Mr Willett said soberly as they both sat. "I have been intrigued to see your estate." The Widow Simmons was not known as a warm and fuzzy hostess, so he was curious and amused by her reaching out to reciprocate Charlotte's invitation. Mr Willett wondered if he was being targeted for a potential matrimonial alliance. He was not averse to the idea, should the right sort of person come along.

"My grounds are quite extensive... ten acres in all. Perhaps you would like to return at another time and enjoy a tour in daylight. An estate such as this is a large undertaking. Staff never take as much care as if it was their own home though."

"This is true. This is true..."

"Do you have a hobby, Mr Willett?" she asked as she put her book to the side.

"Oh well... I... I like to..." He scrambled in his head to find an appropriate response. Truth be known, he didn't have many interests outside estate business and monitoring the activities of his daughter. He caught sight of her book as she put it down. "Like you, I enjoy reading..."

"Yes, I do like to read... and as I suggested, I enjoy walking in my garden and through the grounds. Oh, I forgot to mention, I have my nephew visiting at the moment. Now, he is someone who has a curious hobby... and he wanted to demonstrate it for your pleasure this evening. I hope you would not mind. He was quite insistent. Would you like to guess?"

"His hobby, you say. Does he play music... some of the masters perhaps? Charlotte here, used to play the pianoforte."

"He does enjoy music... the violin, but that is not it."

"Does he play cards?" Charlotte suggested.

"He does... but again, that is not it."

Mr Willett frowned. "Does he want us to do a sitting for an oil painting?"

"No, you are spared a stony-faced portrait sitting."

"Card tricks... the magician's sleight-of-hand is popular in some circles." Charlotte started to laugh but quickly coughed, smothering her amusement in her kerchief.

"Ahh... no... not that I know of. Which is something of a relief," Aunt Prudence frowned. Mr Willett was perhaps as dull as his daughter was reputed to be. He stubbornly refused to be herded into the stockyards not unlike the stupid sheep on the stations in the valley.

"I concur, I concur, Mrs Simmons. If we were to be subjected to that, all the reports of your sensible and practical hospitality would be a complete fabrication."

"I think my point is proven. My nephew has an obscure and unusual hobby. He likes to dabble as a chef. Yes, you did hear me correctly... he likes to experiment with cooking. Which is, as you note, a very sensible and practical pastime to allow, because it means I have an ongoing arrangement of delicacies to tempt my guests. But tonight... he is going one further. Not just petit fours, and other curious appetizers... tonight... he wants to serve a full course meal. Would you be agreeable to that? I know that seems like an unusual way to amuse oneself, but he is my kin, so I am obliged to accommodate his peculiar whims. And he was so eager to please. Rather like a full blood Bassett Hound. I believe a man of your discernment, would be accommodating of the diversity of some gentlemen's pastimes."

Mr Willett raised his brow... and raised them higher during the length of Aunt Prudence's disclosure. But regardless of the lack of convention, she seemed proud of her nephew, and he wanted to stay aligned with her good graces. "Well, well, it sounds entertaining at least, and..." He softened his voice, and leant over in a conspiring whisper, "and we will not let him know of our disappointment at all. We will be delighted with all his efforts."

"Oh, Mr Willett, thank you. I knew I could rely on you both. I would not ask such a familiar request of just anyone. And I knew, as we met again last... that you are people of discerning tastes and manners. To accommodate my nephew's whim like this... it is so very much appreciated. He will be joining us of course... and you must excuse the gravy smears on his cravat. He aligns with those very modern ideas that would presume food falls into the category of virtuosity. Have you heard the latest declaration? *'Cooking is the ultimate form of art'?* In my mind, why not stick to the usual mediums of paint and canvas? To be honest, I would be more comfortable with the smell of turpentine and oil pigments. Still, no accounting for some people's caprices. So, let us see what he comes up with. Please... I know you said you would be courteous and say nothing, but I think... because I trust you so implicitly, we can consider that we are in a gallery... a culinary display of fine art. Give Seth's art at least some form of critique. There is no need to wait until the end of the evening."

Mr Willett held his raised brow high. "Well, Charlotte, what do you think? I think this evening just became surprisingly amusing. You have an extraordinary gift for interesting hospitality, Mrs Simmons."

Aunt Prudence smiled so very amiably; her mask positioned impeccably. "Oh look, here is my nephew now..." Simmons walked into the drawing room, smartly dressed in a dinner suit, no signs of gravy on his cravat, no cooking bandana around his thick dark hair, which flopped with just the right amount of boyish charm. "Mr Willett, let me introduce to you my nephew, Seth Greenwood. He is our artist for this evening."

"Sir, I am delighted to make your acquaintance. And this is...?"

"My daughter, Charlotte."

Simmons paused and smiled and lent over her hand. "Charmed..."

She blushed prettily in return, "A pleasure to meet you, Mr... Greenwood," and Mr Willett raised his brow even higher.

Simmons stood up, tall and stately. "Has my aunt intimated the Bill of Fare for your dining pleasure tonight?"

"Seth, I have suggested that tonight our dining room is like walking into a culinary art-gallery... and you are the artist. Why would I extinguish the anticipation by destroying the element of surprise?"

"I trust all the anticipation will meet with your approval. Shall we dine? Mr Willett, if you would be so kind as to escort my aunt to the dining room. Miss Charlotte...?" And he held out his arm. She took his arm, and he placed his gloved hand over hers and pressed it reassuringly. They paused at the door to allow Mr Willett and Aunt Prudence to pass through to the dining room.

The long table had been removed and a smaller round table was arranged with an exquisite setting for four. Simmons drew out Charlotte's chair and then sat opposite his aunt. "Tonight, of course, we start with soup..." He lifted up his gloved hand and indicated for the staff to start serving.

Four individual soup tureens were served. As they lifted the lids, there was a gasp of surprise from Charlotte and Mr Willett. A basic white soup was swirled with streaks of colours from complimentary soups. Charlotte seemed excited. "How beautiful! I was thinking there was nothing to be done with soup. How did you achieve these colours? It really looks like a painting. An art gallery indeed!"

Mr Willett stared at his daughter curiously. Would soup stir her interest, where nothing else could?

Simmons did not hurry in describing his dish. "The test is in the tasting, Miss Charlotte. Perhaps hold your reviews until you taste it. Can you distinguish what the added soups are? And tell me, are they a compatible combination for the discerning taste palate, or just an interesting colour palette?"

Charlotte picked up her spoon and tasted every selection. "Well, let me see... the base Blancmange is smooth, and the chicken flavour is subtle... a beautiful neutral base for the accents of deep red, bright orange, and fresh green, which are from... beets... pumpkin... broccoli – no, I believe simple green peas." She said it with great satisfaction as if she had unlocked a very complex puzzle. "Beautifully done Si...Seth!"

Mr Willett choked on a mouthful of soup and dabbed his lips with his napkin. "I concur, I concur... *Mister* Greenwood. A delicious starter. You have done well."

Simmons smiled. "Can I ask? Are you being genuine, Sir, or just polite? I am secure enough to take an honest opinion. Every artist improves with reviews and critiques."

Mr Willett frowned. "Hmm. I was quite prepared to be courteous out of veneration of our esteemed hostess, but it seems there was no need to be concerned. This soup is satisfactory, on presentation, and palate. We can be very confident in asserting that the soup in the gallery dining room is an excellent example of your art young man."

He nodded his acceptance of the compliment and steered the conversation to more mundane topics. Prudence added her considered opinion with just enough controversy to keep it interesting without offending anyone.

When the soup tureens were cleared, a red wine was poured, and the next course was presented. On the plates were individual crocks crafted from a small cob of bread, complete with handle and lid. As they lifted the crusty bread lid, the wonderful smell of rich venison stew wafted up; the vegetable sides of small potatoes and asparagus, sat around it. "Oh Father... look! Venison stew is a favourite of yours. Tell me, does this rendition match your fondness for the dish?"

Mr Willette's much-loved dish was not shamed, and he demanded the recipe be sent to their cook. "I am gratified that you approve, Sir," said Simmons as their plates were cleared for the next course. "I have chosen to forgo the usual cheese and salads, for a sweeter conclusion to our meal. I believe this new trend does satisfy a contented appetite. And I have it on a particular authority that this might be a favourite. A good friend gave it a solid review, and this was from a family, highly esteemed in social circles."

That endorsement was sufficient for Mr Willett to deviate from the tradition of cheese and salad, and a Homestead Baklava was presented on a crystal cake stand. There was an explanation of the exotic Turkish dish used as the inspiration for the favourite Australian flavours for the rich dessert. It sounded complicated and considered and continental... so all in all, that made it an acceptable experiment. Mr Willett was an unconfessed closet sweet-tooth, and although he didn't rave, there were subtle signs of dining pleasure that leaked out. Charlotte enjoyed every mouthful. It took her back to the Redwood kitchen bench, where she sat, perched on a stool, with a silver cake fork. She smiled and nodded enthusiastically as Simmons adjusted her chair as she stood up to be escorted back to the drawing room. "Mr Greenwood, you have excelled on every level. I have thoroughly enjoyed our visit to your gallery this evening. It is a shame that you keep your art hidden. It is like you are depriving a whole community of your art."

He smiled at her on his arm. "My satisfaction right now is that you have enjoyed our tour. Thank you for allowing me to show you around," he said as his aunt and Mr Willett settled back into the drawing room armchairs with hot tea and some after-dinner sweet petit fours.

"Masterpieces each one," declared Mr Willett, and he leaned over and took another sweet from the plate. He lowered his voice. "There really is no need to be ashamed of your young nephew's bizarre fascination with his art. Although the form is unconventional, he does it with such style that very few would even notice his eccentric attraction to it."

Aunt Prudence glanced over to Simmons who was encouraging Charlotte to play the pianoforte. "I suspect someone else has noticed the attraction," she said with a knowing smile.

Mr Willett turned and gasped as he saw them both standing at the piano. Simmons was adjusting the lamp light and setting out the pages of sheet music for Charlotte, who was charming him with a smile. "It is only fair. I have shared my art... now you must offer some of yours," they heard him say. "Music is the only appropriate way to conclude a social evening such as this," he said.

"Mrs Simmons, your young man will be disappointed. Charlotte has refused to play music since her mother passed. I really don't think that she will accommodate him."

"Perhaps not. It seems she is resisting Seth's appeal to showcase her talent. Or..." They watched as Charlotte turned and sat, blushing. "It now looks very much that she might..." She began to gently play a Beethoven favourite.

"Ohhh..." Mr Willett's face melted as he watched, with affection, Charlotte caressing the ivory keys. "Oh, how I have missed Charlotte's playing. Your nephew... Ma'am... your nephew has offered me a great service. I am so very grateful. So very grateful. He has brought music back into my daughter's life." And he cleared his throat and sipped his port... and ate another sweet, blinking hard in the dimness of the room where they sat.

As they took their leave, Simmons handed Mr Willett his card. "I would be obliged if I could call, Sir. Miss Charlotte tells me that you have a beautiful pianoforte at your home, and that she would be inclined to play some Chopin."

"Well, well. In service to my daughter's preference, I think that would be permittable."

As the door closed, Aunt Prudence paused and rolled her eyes. Simmons looked at her with a frown. "What? I didn't think that went too badly. I have secured permission to go calling, so your influence is well on the way to achieving its end."

"Nothing wrong with my influence, but you seem entirely too eager. Bassett Hound is right. My goodness! You are slobbering all over him like an excited little house-pet. Show some reserve and restraint. Decorum is required. You are blue-collar passing yourself off as a gold-lapel. We fared reasonably well... but there is more to be done."

⁂

19.

With the enlistment of some particular high-profile figures, who managed some strategic name dropping in certain circles, Mrs Simmons ensured her nephew, Seth Greenwood, suddenly developed a respectable social profile. People were curious about this wandering sheep from the Simmons family fold who would emerge out of the fog to go calling at the Grosvenor estate. Simmons took with him a couple of sweet options for her father's occasional dining pleasure to enjoy with his afternoon tea. Charlotte did play Chopin on the pianoforte, and Mr Willett agreed to Mr Greenwood returning, if just to hear his daughter play again.

On the third visit, Mr Willett ushered Simmons into his library and poured them both a stiff port. Simmons looked at it cautiously and took it without comment. Mr Willett stared at him severely and didn't even offer a seat. He took a rather undignified swig of his drink. "Dempsey came to see me yesterday. He said you are a common pubcook, stepping outside your designation by daring to call on my daughter. He said he saw you working at Redwood Inn, when he went up to the goldfields."

Simmons looked at him evenly and took a drink. Then he shrugged. "Research," he said dismissively.

"Research? What are you talking about? Did he see you there or not?"

"Yes, he saw me. I was engaging in research for my craft. It might shock you to know I have also researched in a drover's camp and a shearing shed. If I am able to satisfy such unapologetic appetites it gives credence to my skill, not otherwise. Do you know those who enjoy a spot of shooting? They would never allow others to pull the trigger for them. They insist on going bush, enduring all sorts of hardships, to experience the hunt and hit their mark, in person."

"Humph. Research. Of course. I wasn't too worried. The man is just eating sour grapes because Charlotte turned him down. Obviously, he would try to discredit you." He took another drink. "So, what I do need to know, young man, is… what are your intentions? The fact remains, that when her previous engagement did not flourish, my daughter was on the verge of joining a nunnery. Her delicate constitution needs to be considered, and I will not have you behaving in a way that is going to push her toward taking vows that will never allow our family to see another generation."

"Really. A convent?" Nothing Martha ever said, indicated that she was contemplating a life of contemplation.

"She cut her hair! Everyone knows that is the first phase of admission to a religious life. Her good nature is fragile, and the Willett blood is our legacy. She has changed since you are here, but if you don't intend an honourable proposal, I must insist you stop calling."

"Sir, it would not be seemly to rush these matters of the heart in the manner of an untamed puppy. My intentions are not aligned with puppy love… but something more enduring." How much should he say? Aunt Prudence insisted he must not seem too eager.

"Then ask me for her hand and secure the matter. Charlotte is getting on. And although she is determined to be content to live out her days on her father's arm, the matter of her marriage is an important consideration."

"Very well, Sir... I respectfully ask for your daughter's hand in marriage."

"Done. Now where will you live?"

"What do you mean?"

"I mean that you need an appropriate residence to accommodate my daughter." But before Simmons could formulate a response, Mr Willett moved on. "I propose that you reside here... in the East Wing. It is close to the kitchen so you can amuse yourself with your art. If it is not to your satisfaction, we can upgrade it with whatever modern newfangled gadgets you need. It would not be a difficult thing to have you practice your venison stew now and then."

"Oh. Has Charlotte suggested this is her preference?"

"Sometimes, young man, it is necessary that we let the women know what their preference is."

"Oh. Well, I do know she is very much devoted to you, so this is something to consider." He was hedging.

"And what else do you need?"

"What else do I need for what?"

"To get this consensus turned into a wedding!"

"Do you have a particular time frame in mind?" Suddenly, it seemed to Simmons, that he was marrying her father.

"I spoke with your aunt. She is very enthusiastic about Charlotte. She is of the mind that if you are tardy, it would be unseemly. Delay would feed any controversy related to your sudden appearance in society. Given that you have been traveling away to date, it is time to demonstrate your stability by settling down.”

“Oh. So would a six-month betrothal seem appropriate to you?”

“Grief man! Three at the most. Two would be better.”

“Is there something I don’t know? This seems rushed.”

“See! There it is. Your Aunt confided that you would be reluctant, but I was reassured by your attentive manners and devotion. Perhaps I was wrong.”

“You are not wrong. I am determined to marry Charlotte. I would marry her tomorrow if I thought there was a way to do that with deference to your station. But I will be guided by your wisdom and choose two months. Given she accepts my proposal, of course.”

“Of course, she will. She is besotted! But she has no head for practical matters, or else she would have already secured your commitment. Now I have one other request of you.” He put down his stout stemmed glass and went to his desk. He unlocked a small compartment with a key and pulled out a ring box. “I would like you to use her mother’s ring.” Inside was a generous rose cut diamond ring, freshly cleaned and he sat it on his desk. It seemed to get larger and larger, staring him down with its unblinking eye.

“Have I completely misjudged you or do I need to supervise this as well?” Mr Willett asked impatiently. He tinkled a bell on his desk. “Mary, ask Charlotte to come here to the library.” He turned as she left to do his bidding. “Take a firm hand... or you will find she will waver in knowing her own mind.”

Charlotte came in and paused at the door as she saw them standing there. She took in the port glasses with their contents drained. She noticed the ring box... and the uncertain look on Simmons face.

"Sir. Could I please have a private audience with your daughter... alone..."

He patted Simmons shoulder as he walked past, and mouthed the words, "Firm hand," as he left.

Simmons frowned and indicated for Charlotte to take a seat. "This is not at all what I expected, Little Martha. I need your wisdom... because right now, it seems I have been asked to marry your father and not you at all."

"What do you mean? I have been giving him all the signals of my devotion to you. I thought he would be convinced of my sentiments."

"But that is just it. He is. He has directed me to propose – immediately; he has specifically asked for only a two-month engagement; he wants us to live in the East wing so I can cook his favourite venison stew; and he has asked that I use your mother's engagement ring for our betrothal. And although I wanted his consent... this has thrown me. You said I would know when and where, to make a proposal, but I didn't know any of this! Is this what your life is like? Do you have no autonomy at all? This morning's interview has been the most unmanning experience of my life. I would rather do battle with Aunt Prudence, to be honest."

"Ahh. That makes sense."

"It does? Because I am not making sense of any of this."

"Aunt Prudence. My father is someone who is keen to please. He wants to please me... he knows I regard you well. But is it possible that Aunt Prudence, with all her flattery and influence, has convinced him that he needs to be so directive because you would not know your own mind? Is he trying to please her?"

"Of course! Yes. Aunt Prudence. Your father said that I needed to demonstrate stability and act quickly to forestall any controversy. Yes, you are right: this has Aunt Prudence's fingerprints all over it. Influence... but with her back handed insults enmeshed all the way through it. It was presented in such an unfamiliar form; I didn't recognise it. You are a discerning woman, Little Martha."

"Well thank you, Sir. You asked if this is my life. You know me well enough to know I won't have my hand forced where I don't want it forced. But sometimes I allow others the room to think they have taken the initiative so things can be smoother. The battle for me is usually working out whether this is a matter I want to batten down the hatches for."

"So, in this, what would you do battle for?"

"I would fight for you. But I already have you. So that is not needed. I like the idea of a short engagement. So, I am in agreement with Father on that. Wearing my mother's ring? It is not a fashionable cut, but it is classically tasteful. I miss my mother so much and this sentiment allows that she would be part of my wedding in a way that I will otherwise not have the opportunity for. I would very much like to wear it."

"And living here?"

"Hmm. My father can be smothering. I'm none too concerned for myself because I am used to his ways, and I generally have my own means of getting around that. But you, Simmons... you are used to the open plains of Drovers' camps and sheep stations with shearing sheds. Would you be comfortable here?"

"See, little Martha, this is what makes you an exceptional woman. I think we could make it work. He has already given me licence to access the kitchen. Since I don't have to cook Bully Stew and damper, I can spend more time on the things that I love. I could develop a line of desserts to supply cafés around. Perhaps you would consider continuing your mother's charitable legacy... and you may need to hire a caterer for those events. I have experience in mundane Roman fare. Perhaps life can be brought back into this quiet old house after all."

"See, Simmons... the light has turned back on in your eyes. You have found your own flavour in this. This is you adapting to more of the changing faces of the Australian landscape. Father need never know that we discussed this like grown-ups, and I am perfectly fine that he thinks that I sat here and allowed you to tell me my mind. In a way, he might find that reassuring."

"So, you still wear your masks, Little Martha?"

"No, only Charlotte wears a mask. It is always expected. But Little Martha has the privilege of being able to see and truly be seen. That is the gift you have given me, Simmons. With you, I am safe enough to allow my mask to drop."

He swiped the ring box from the table and knelt in front of her chair. "Little Martha, will you marry me? Will you take a short engagement, and wear your mother's ring and live with me here in your father's home?" He grinned. "That would have to be the world's most pathetic proposal. But what do you say? Will we let your father know that I have convinced your mind?"

"Yes, I will marry you, Simmons. I know it is not a romantic proposal that has secured my heart. It has been those points of honest connection over roast duck, and on the dance floor, or behind Lazarus' grave clothes. There is nothing more desirable than truly being seen. Simmons, my promise to you is that I will wear no masks between us. You see me as I truly am."

"Little Martha, I love what I see! I love that you see me as I am. I love you." And he slid the ring over her finger and drew her in for a kiss.

Coming soon from Olwyn Harris: Pioneers of Grace Series

Book 5 – Crucible of Grace

Ruth has had more than her fair share of tragedy. When her widowed mother-in-law wants to return to the farming region where her family once thrived, Ruth works as a laundry maid to support them. Can Ruth survive the fire of heartache and prejudice to find a new shape for her life, which might even include the station owner?

Book 6 – Sculpture of Grace

Rachel loves her country life. She loves her art of forging iron and her growing friendship with the station's newest blacksmith. Leah, her older sister, on the other hand, does not like anything country. But, as fate would have it, Rachel is offered a proposal which means she would have to leave the valley she loves, while Leah is sidelined and mourns her dreams of more. Can the sisters find a way to reconcile their destinies and forge a different story where they both see their dreams come true?

Book 1 - Time of Grace

Abigail is the elegant wife of the most powerful station-owner in the valley. But powerful also means brutish and cruel. To correct her husband's crimes, Abby is drawn into contact with the disgraced lawyer Ruben Davey, hiding in the hills with a band of displaced bushrangers. Will Abby be able to address these injustices and find a way to navigate towards a safer future in the meantime?

Book 2 - Circle of Grace

All her life Hannah had been sensible and sincere. When her humble circumstances lead her to work as the companion for Lady Whitmore, she is confronted with Lady Whitmore's nephew, the most shallow and irresponsible man she has ever met. As their life of privilege collapses around them, will she follow Lady Whitmore and Sebastian to Australia, to explore a new life in exile?

Book 3 - Journey of Grace

Tibby had grand dreams that were very different from the squalor of the textile mill tenements where she grew up. She plotted her escape by taking sponsored passage to the Colony as a bride, but everything on this journey was harder than even she could imagine. Dumped like garbage at the gate of Zachary Logan's place, will it be possible for Tabitha to sew a new life together in this barren wasteland of Australia?

#1 The Beachside Cottage

In this offering from Olwyn Harris, we meet the heartbroken and downtrodden Eliza-Beth Perkins. Eliza-Beth is facing the dire consequences of her choices and the possibility of life in the poorhouse. Then she, literally, runs into Jensen Harker. Jensen is facing his own heartbreak at the death of his wife and wants nothing more than to be left alone. But something in Eliza-Beth stirs him to make a rash proposal, thus rescuing her from her predicament. As we follow their journey together, will we see them find the healing they both desperately need?

#2 Petrea Downs

In the 2nd book in this series, we meet Meg. Meg's life has been turned upside-down, with her husband gone, trying to run Petrea Downs by herself, and disaster after disaster at every turn. Thankfully, her neighbour Everett Grossman is always there to help. The final blow comes when a cattle duffer tries to steal her only source of income, gets shot, and has to be nursed back to health in her living room. But, is Ben Harker really the villain he seems? And is Everett really the hero he makes himself out to be?

#3 The Writer's Retreat

The third book in the Homes of Healing trilogy introduces us to Tess, a romance writer, who prides herself on letting her characters tell their own story. When she arrives at Rocky Creek B&B, the run-down stone cottage looks like the perfect place for her to retreat to, not only to write her book, but to escape her past. Join her as she discovers her characters and explores their stories and finds that God is intent on becoming part of her own story at the same time. As her relationship with the local publican challenges her to stop running, she realises that real life and real love can be messy and complicated. Can she honestly confront the ugly aspects in her own story, so that God can bring them both to a place of healing?

#1 Sapphires of Hope

"There is no way," she thought, "that I am going to use this!" She had desperately searched their cupboards for something, anything that would come close to what she needed for her catering project. She found only this old dilapidated breadbasket that looked like the sort of junk that comes from one of those tacky jumble-sale stalls..." Andi and Jo are best friends... they do pretty much everything together. So, when Andi has a catering assignment due, and only a tacky old basket to use, Jo helps her pull off the faded decorations, revealing a time-capsule of historical information, and in order to understand what it means, Andi and Jo ask their elderly neighbour to take them to visit the farm where the basket came from. They find themselves dumped back in history at the time of Federation, embroiled in circumstances that nearly cost Andi her life and threatens the livelihood of the people living there. How can they ever hope to keep going when things are spinning out of control?

#2 Rubies of Ambition

In the 2nd book in the Gem of Australia series, we again travel with Andi and Jo back in time. On this adventure, they meet the very beautiful and ambitious actress, Lillian Browning, who is on the run from the federal police. Andi and Jo accompany her back to her hometown, where they find she is not well received. Will Lillian find a balance between the past that calls her and the ambitions that drive her?

#3 Emerald Dreams

In the third installment of the *Gems of Australia* series, Olwyn Harris brings Australian history to life as she takes us on a journey back to the early days of convict settlement in Australia. Here we, once again, find Andi and Jo learning about Australia's true history, and finding strength in God to help others.

#1: **A Spacious Place**

In this first instalment of the Guthrie's Lot series, set in the late 1800s, we meet Irvin Guthrie, a practical, no-nonsense man with a sick wife and a small child to care for. When his wife's doctor suggests they move to a warmer climate, he spends everything he has on a property that ends up not being what he expected.

Joanna Grenham has dreams of being a schoolteacher. When an opportunity presents itself, she jumps at the chance, only to find herself given no choice but to care for Irvin's sick wife and child.

Will Irvin and Joanna make the most of their circumstances, or will they forever find life as hard and unyielding as the ground in A Spacious Place.

#2: **A Level Path**

In the second instalment of the Guthrie's Lot series, it is now the late 1960s. Here we meet Irvin's granddaughter Iris. Iris hungers for excitement and adventure, and she won't find that in Gumleigh, or with the ever-predictable Dave. The last thing she expected was for Dave to follow her across the world to England as she tries to find direction and meaning.

Will Iris finally see through the charismatic, but ultimately selfish, Stan, or will Dave leave England alone and leave Iris to find her own way to A Level Path?

#3: **The Crying Tree**

In this final episode of the Guthrie's Lot series, the year is now 2010. We meet Mac, who has always been an achiever – a do-er, just like her father. After the death of her mother, she finds that she needs to get away, so she buys a little run-down stone cottage in the middle of nowhere to transform into a creative studio. She is taken by the feel of the place - especially the twisted weeping willow tree behind the house, even though it doesn't fit into her plans anywhere.

Dan spent years growing up on the old Guthrie place, so when the new owner arrives, he is not convinced that he wants to work for this headstrong woman, who is obviously used to getting what she wants, but he feels that it is something he has to do – and only God knows why.

Can Dan and Mac work together to make her dreams into a reality? Will she transform the old Guthrie place, and her life, into something unique and beautiful? And what will become of The Crying Tree.

Matt's Boys of Wattle Creek

When Matthew Lawson's three sons were born, he wrote each of them a letter outlining his hopes and prayers for their futures. When he decided to give up his city job and move to the little town of Wattle Creek, he could never have imagined the effect it would have on his young family. As Matt's boys grow to maturity and find their places in their community, will his dreams and prayers come to fulfilment? Will his boys develop their own faith in the eternal God? And will they each find the kind of love that Matt holds for his beautiful Josie?

Maggie & Minotaur

"For Maggie, the mythical Minotaur represented Romance – half man, half beast. The Minotaur was a monster created from centuries of classical Greek mythology and no normal man could withstand its strength...... Sooner or later she would accept that Theseus, the hero, did not exist. She knew that she would have to battle through the maze of reality and confront it herself...." Maggie Wick was shipped off to the city and high society life at the age of 12, where she would learn the ways of the rich and marry into a family of influence. What could have caused her sudden return to Henderson's Gap? Can she really settle back into life on the station, with all its diversity and challenges? Will she find fulfilment in her role as provisional schoolteacher? Will she ever figure out the "Captain", the mysterious, intimidating, station manager? When war comes to her little haven and Maggie's world comes crashing down, taking her loved ones and the captain with it, Maggie needs to find a way to survive. Will her faith be enough to protect her, and what of the Captain? Could he really be the Theseus who would do battle with her Minotaur?

The Bush Olympics
The Bush Olympics, written by Olwyn Harris and beautifully illustrated by Shelly Askew, shows us that we don't have to be good at everything to be part of a team. Even sleepy Koala is good at something, and if everyone plays their part, we can all be successful together.